M000073747

CLAIMED BY GODS

THEIR DARK VALKYRIE #1

EVA CHASE

INK SPARK PRESS

Claimed by Gods

Book 1 in the Their Dark Valkyrie series

All rights reserved. This book or any portion thereof may not be
reproduced or used in any manner without the express written
permission of the author, except for the use of brief quotations in a book
review.

This is a work of fiction. Any resemblance to actual persons, living or
dead, or actual events is purely coincidental.

First Digital Edition, 2018

Copyright © 2018 Eva Chase

Cover design: Rebecca Frank

Ebook ISBN: 978-1-989096-11-6

Paperback ISBN: 978-1-989096-12-3

❀ Created with Vellum

1

_____

Aria

I'd like to tell you that I died in epic fashion, guns blazing in the middle of a vast street brawl, or at least something scandalously hot, like falling off a balcony during the most incredible sex of my life. The truth? My death was cringingly mundane.

I hopped off my moped on the grungy Philly street and loped across the road to the doggy daycare where a client was waiting. The blazing July sun made the asphalt stink, and chances were ten to one the guys on the corner had crack and pistols underneath those baggy jerseys. It was hard to say which was more dangerous: the neighborhood or the package stashed in my shoulder bag. A well-paid courier doesn't ask what she's carrying; she just delivers the goods on time.

One of the toughs whose name I'd never had to learn stood behind the front desk, and Gene was leaning against the wall nearby. Oh joy. He straightened up and gave me a greasy smile as I tugged the taped-up parcel out of my bag.

"Ari. Always a pleasure."

"Wish I could say the same, Gene," I said brightly, handing the parcel over to the tough. He examined it with a brisk nod and reached under the desk to get my money. Whines and yips emanated from the inner room where their few doggy charges hung out, providing a front for whatever their real business was. I didn't ask questions about that stuff.

Gene blinked at me. I'd learned a long time ago that you could be as insultingly honest as you'd like as long as you made the words sound cheery enough. Brains like his just didn't know how to process both the meaning and the tone at the same time.

Unfortunately, the dimness of his brain also meant he never gave up on hitting on me, even though he was old enough to be my dad and so smarmy I doubt I'd have had the slightest interest when he'd been in his twenties either. He was also the cousin of one of my biggest clients, so I couldn't just stab him a few times to get the point across, as much as I'd sometimes wanted to.

Not fatally, of course. Just somewhere painful enough that message would stick.

Instead, when he sidled over to me and tried to put his arm around my waist, I had to simply dodge to the side, pasting a stiff smile on my face. My hand dropped to the pocket of my jeans, taking comfort in tracing the lump of the switchblade I *would* use if I absolutely had to.

"Aw, come on, honey," Gene said. "You can't come in here lookin' like that and deny a guy a little fun. I'd show you a good time."

I had on my jeans—fitted but not *that* tight—and a loose white T-shirt with a neckline that barely grazed my collarbone. No makeup, my shoulder-length blond hair rumpled from the moped ride. By *looking like that* he meant existing while young and female.

"I'm sure you would, Gene," I said, still smiling. "And I could show you my fist breaking your nose. But I think it's probably better if we avoid all that and just stay friends, huh?"

Gene put his puzzled face on again. He took another shuffle at me, and I raised that fist, arching an eyebrow.

"Three-time high school boxing champion," I added. "You really want to try me?" My voice was still sweet, but I let a hint of a glare harden my gaze.

Gene took me in and decided that backing off was in the best interest of maintaining his delusion that I'd be chomping at the bit for him any day now.

I'd never actually boxed in my life, but I'd landed enough effective punches that it didn't feel like a total lie.

The tough finally handed over my damn envelope. I flicked through the bills, tossed a "Thank you!" at him, and stuffed the money in my bag as I headed out the door.

It was a good payout, and I'd already done a decent run this week. I could pick up something for Petey this weekend. Not half the things I wanted to get him, since it had to be small enough that Mom wouldn't notice. A pack of those trading cards he was hooked on, and some snacks—maybe better shoes to replace the ratty sneakers she should have realized he'd grown out of? If I dirtied them up some first, she might not realize they were new...

Picturing my little brother's grinning face was the best antidote for Gene's unwelcome attention. A real smile crossed my face, but at the same time my heart squeezed.

Trading cards and shoes weren't enough. Nothing was going to be enough while Mom was... the way she was. If Petey's life there turned into even half the nightmare mine had been...

I shook those thoughts away. I was doing everything I could despite her. I wouldn't *let* anyone hurt him. And as soon as I'd saved up enough to get a nice house and the sharpest lawyer in the city, I'd fight until he could live under my roof instead.

The hooky beat of a pop song spilled from the open doorway of the mini-mart next door. A little sway crept into my stride as I made for my moped. Maybe I'd go dancing tonight, blow off some steam before I was pounding the street again. It'd been a while.

I wasn't looking left as I walked across, because it was a one-way street. But just as I hit the middle of the road, a yellow jeep came roaring around the corner, faster than any sane person should have been driving even going the right way.

The driver gave a shout. The tires screeched. I threw myself toward the opposite sidewalk.

Which might have saved me, if the guy behind the wheel hadn't been so high he decided to try to avoid me by veering in the same direction I was going.

4

The grill slammed into my side with a sickening crunch I heard as well as felt. Agony exploded all through my body. My legs crumpled. The corner of the bumper bashed my head with a skull-splitting *crack*.

The jumbled noises around me were swallowed up by a wave of pain. As my vision shrank to a pinhole and the light contracted with it, I had enough consciousness left to think, *Fucking jackass and his fucking jackass jeep.* And then, *Who's going to take care of Petey? He won't even know why I'm gone.*

A sharper, frantic jab of distress cut through the surging pain. But it wasn't enough to keep me there.

The wave crashed through me and over me and pulled me under, down into the dark where there was simply nothing.

———

Eyelids twitched.

My eyelids twitched.

Awareness crept through my body from there, sensation prickling through numbness across my cheeks and forehead, down my neck and over my chest and limbs.

I *had* limbs. I had a chest. A chest that was no longer a flaming mass of pain.

My head was still foggy. I blinked, and colors swam before my eyes. A chill tingled over my skin and my back felt weirdly heavy, but otherwise I didn't seem to be in bad shape. Had someone gotten me to a hospital?

Maybe it was drugs making my mind and my vision so loopy.

I blinked again, and the colors merged into shapes. The shapes moved. Two of them, close by, came into focus.

Two men, both tall and muscular, though one was as beefy as anything with dark auburn hair and the other leanly slim, his hair pale red. And those perfectly chiseled faces, broad and square-jawed on one and gracefully angular on the other... If this was a hospital, it was more like the Hollywood movie set version.

Both of them were peering at me intently. Beefy took another step closer, holding out a white sheet as if to give it to me. To *me*? Because...

My awareness sharpened, my mind settling deeper into my body. Into my lightly chilled skin, which was chilled because I was wearing nothing over it. I was lying completely naked on some kind of padded surface in the middle of this big yellow room, with two strange men twice as big as me looming closer.

An icy jab of panic shot through my nerves. My arms and legs jerked as I got control of them through my daze. I scrambled against the floor, pushing myself away from the two men.

No, not just two. There were two others standing farther back, and a woman also, all of them watching me. The strange drag on my back made me wobble as I pulled my legs under me, bracing my hands and feet against the floor.

"Hey, there," Beefy said in a rumbling baritone, shaking the sheet as if to tempt me with it. As if I were a dog he was beckoning with a treat. "It's all right. No one here is going to hurt you."

Uh, yeah right. Because you could always trust *anyone* who made promises like that.

"What the fuck is going on?" I said, hunching lower to cover myself. "Where the hell am I?"

"Quite a different experience from the other ones, isn't she?" Slim glanced around at the others, his voice lightly amused. His gaze came back to me, and he cocked his head. "A little smaller than I realized she'd be. A regular pixie."

I had no clue what the hell he was talking about, but I knew I didn't like that comment. I gritted my teeth, the muscles in my shoulders flexing. "Just try me."

"And such spirit!" He grinned as if he expected me to join in the joke.

"Give her time to adjust," Beefy said. "We've got to let her get comfortable." He frowned, motioning with the sheet again. "Are you sure you don't want this?"

"I want you to tell me how I got here and what the fuck you think you're doing," I said.

My gaze darted past them and landed on a door at the far end of the room. I could make a run for it. They were stronger and bigger than me, sure, but I was fast. And they didn't seem to be expecting me to bolt, so I'd have surprise on my side.

"That's a little complicated," Slim said. "Why don't you relax and get your bearings for a minute, and then we can get into the nitty gritty details?"

A rough laugh burst out of my throat. Relax? Was he kidding?

I looked to the woman again—almost as tall as the guys and just as striking in looks, her face smooth as a supermodel's amid her waves of honey-brown hair. Who the hell *were* these people?

Would she help me, or was she planning on leaving me to the mercy of these men? Or on joining in with whatever they had planned?

She stared back at me, her mouth tightening. I thought I saw sympathy in her expression, but she didn't speak, didn't budge an inch.

I was on my own then.

The other guys were still hanging back near the room's big arched windows. Not too close to the door. Beefy took another step toward me.

How long until he forced the issue? I had to get out of here, and I had to go *now*. I shoved myself forward off the polished hardwood.

If my body had been working properly, that effort would have propelled me halfway across the room in just a few quick strides. But my shoulder blades twinged as if something had yanked on them and that weight on my back threw me to the side. What the hell was hanging off of me?

My shoulder glanced off the wall. Slim was in front of me in an instant, blocking the way. He was still fucking *smiling*.

My fist swung out, more out of instinct than because any part of me thought I had a chance in a hand to hand fight with him, and he outright laughed. I teetered backward and fumbled at my back in an attempt to detach whatever was dragging on me. My fingers brushed a softly rippled surface that my mind couldn't make any sense of.

Beefy closed in on me from the other side, brandishing that damned sheet. "Fuck off!" I said in what was practically a snarl. I dodged to the side, and Slim followed, his eyes sparkling with pleasure.

"Very different from the others," he murmured. "Good, good." He glanced over his shoulder. "Oh, nephew, I think you'd better mellow her out for a bit so we can give introductions another try later."

Mellow me out? One of the other guys, a little shorter than Beefy and Slim but still powerfully built, drifted across the room toward us. Beneath the fall of his shaggy white-blond hair, his eyes were crystal blue and weirdly dreamy. He met my eyes, but his expression didn't give any sign he'd noticed how freaked out I was. A shiver rippled through me.

No. I couldn't let them trap me here. I wouldn't let myself be helpless.

I hurled myself toward the door again, compensating better for the burden on my back now that I was getting used to it. Slim snatched out. But he didn't touch me—at least, not anything that should have been me. A jolt of sensation shot through me to my back, as if he'd grasped onto a limb I hadn't known I had. It jarred me to a stop.

My head spun. None of this made sense. "What the hell did you *do* to me?" I said, lashing out with another fist.

Slim sidestepped neatly, still holding onto that part of my body that shouldn't exist, that never had before. He gave me a smaller smile.

"We made you alive again, pixie," he said. "We made you a valkyrie."

He tugged that alien limb, and then I saw it at the corner of my eye: the unfurling of a huge silver-white feathered wing. A wing his fingers were curled around with a pressure I could feel along the length of it, all the way to where its flesh met my back.

A choked cry broke from my lips, and then the dreamy-eyed man filled my vision. His hands cupped my head. Before I had a chance to struggle, fluffy numbness enveloped my mind, washing the men and the room and all my frantic thoughts away into a warm bright void.

2

Thor

The girl slumped at Baldur's touch, her eyelids sliding shut and her head sagging. I pushed in to catch her before her body hit the floor.

She'd looked so tough a moment ago—small, yes, but wiry with muscle and blazing with rage—that the softness of her slack arms surprised me. I eased her down to the floor and draped the sheet I'd tried to offer her over her. She hadn't liked being naked in front of us. I'd been able to tell that much without her saying it.

Her wings were already shrinking with a faint rustling of the feathers, contracting back into her body where they'd stay until she urged them out again. If she ever got to that point. My mouth twisted as I brushed a lock of her dark blond hair away from her closed eyes.

She looked peaceful now, but she'd been terrified on top of furious a minute ago. *We* had terrified her. Why in

Asgard's name hadn't I been prepared for that? Maybe the ones before had been the strange ones, holding still in their initial confusion, patient enough to hear our story and witness who and what we were.

But humans, all of them, were *my* charges more than that of any of the others here. I was the guardian of humankind. And the last five minutes had been a pretty epic failure of that duty.

Loki came up beside me, rubbing his narrow chin as he studied the girl. His eyes twinkled. "Well, I did promise something different, didn't I? She's a fighter, all right."

"A good one," I allowed. I'd been in enough battles to know experience and skill when I saw it, even in rough mortal form. "Which was promising to see. Of course, it'd have been better if she'd been aiming to fight our enemies and not *us*."

"I'm sure once we've established ourselves and our enemies properly, we can get her on the right track."

"Oh, you're sure, are you?" Hod said where he was standing with arms crossed near the windows. His expression was as dark as his short black hair. "Just like you were sure this 'brilliant' new idea of yours would go off without a hitch? From the moment she came to, it's looked like one giant hitch to me."

The light in Loki's eyes flared momentarily hotter, but he replied in his usual wry tone. "I'd imagine it didn't *look* like anything at all to you."

Hod's scowled deepened. After centuries of practice, he could aim his blind glower based on Loki's voice so accurately you'd almost believe he could see the trickster.

"You know what I mean. Semantics don't change anything."

"If the success of every endeavor were judged by its first five minutes, civilization would be a terribly desolate affair," Loki said breezily.

"She's fine for the moment," Baldur said beside me, his voice as slow and melodic as always. As bright as his twin was dark. "I calmed her mind."

"Right." I pulled my thoughts away from my younger brothers and our trickster companion, back to the matter at hand. "Let's find some way to make her more comfortable so she'll be in a better mood the second time she wakes up."

Freya ambled over and motioned with a graceful arm. "Bring her up to the usual bedroom. We should find her some clothes. Something to eat. And perhaps give her a little time on her own before she has to face the lot of you again?"

Loki chuckled, but he didn't argue. Hod looked happy enough to have the problem taken care of without him, and Baldur... Well, it was hard to tell what Baldur was thinking these days in general. Not a whole lot seemed to penetrate that dreamy glow around him. He didn't look bothered by the suggestion, anyway.

I eased my arms around the girl and lifted her. In sleep, she felt like barely anything. Keeping the sheet tucked around her, I rested her head and shoulders against my much wider shoulder and carried her to the stairs.

Freya followed me up. As I laid the girl on the bed in the room the other valkyries had used for the brief time they'd been with us, the goddess opened the wardrobe and considered its offerings. She took out a white silk blouse and a pair of gray linen slacks, folded them, and set them in a neat pile with various undergarments at the end of the bed. Then she stood and contemplated the girl.

"Do you think we should have listened to him?" I asked. She knew who I meant by *him*.

"Loki has gotten us out of trouble at least as often as he's gotten us into it," she said. "As... questionable as his methods may sometimes be. And it's true our first few tries didn't get us very far."

"Yes." My jaw tightened as I remembered the other young women who'd slept in that bed. Who'd been in our presence for just a few days and then...

We didn't even know for sure what had happened to them. They hadn't come back. That said enough right there.

"If that trickster has ever been loyal to anyone, it's Odin," Freya added. "He wants to find him as much as the rest of us do. I'm sure he wouldn't have suggested anything he suspected would hurt our cause, in any case."

"Point taken." After all the time I'd spent in Loki's presence, all the crazy exploits he'd gotten me wrapped up in over our long lifetimes, I still couldn't say I had any idea how that bizarre but clever mind of his worked. Norns knew I hadn't come up with any brilliant new plans on my end.

The goddess let out a sigh. I glanced over at her, focusing for a moment on her instead of our valkyrie. On the woman I could almost call my stepmother, except that the term felt a little ridiculous when I'd already been several centuries old at the time of the new marriage. Sometimes Odin hardly felt like he could be my father. When he wasn't there in the room with that vast presence of his, anyway.

I should extend some kind of courtesy. As sort-of family, and, well, fellow god stranded here on the human plane. I didn't dislike Freya. We just didn't have a whole lot in common.

"Are you holding up all right?" I said.

Freya's gaze slid to me with an amused twitch of her full lips, as if she could tell how much effort it'd taken me to pick what seemed like the best question. "As well as can be expected, I suppose. It's not as if I'm any stranger to your father's long rambles."

"It's never been quite like this, though."

"No, it hasn't." She shook her head and turned toward the door with a huff. "I'll get those refreshments for her, since apparently the other three in this house can't be bothered."

I didn't know what to do but stand there by the bed as I waited for Freya to come back. A furrow creased the girl's brow. Suddenly she didn't look so peaceful anymore. What else could I do for her that would make her feel safe when she woke up?

I moved the pile of clothes up the bed so she'd see them the moment she opened her eyes. That didn't seem like enough, but nothing else occurred to me.

Freya swept back in with a glass of water and a plate with an apple and crackers. "Just something to tide her over," she said when I raised my eyebrows. "Not everyone can eat a whole roast every hour like the insatiable Thor."

"I'll have you know the most roasts I've ever eaten in one day is five," I said. We wouldn't get into how many *other* things I might have eaten that same day. My stomach grumbled. Maybe I'd better put something in it to hold me over until dinner.

Freya let out a little laugh, and the girl stirred. Her lips parted with a murmured breath, her fingers curling into the pillow I'd rested her head on. The goddess and I both went still.

"We should leave her," Freya said under her breath. "I don't think she's going to be happy to see any of us quite yet."

And just leave the girl alone in this unfamiliar room in an unfamiliar house? My legs balked. But on the other hand, was seeing an unfamiliar person in that room really going to comfort her any?

"All right," I said. "But we've got to make sure we do right by this one."

"We *meant* to do right by all of them," Freya muttered as we slipped out, and a lump settled in my gut that had nothing to do with hunger.

3
_____

Aria

Sunlight seeped through my eyelids. Time to wake up. I opened my eyes cautiously. My heart thudded with a sudden lurch that told me something was wrong.

That thought dredged up a wash of memories: the strange men around me and the glimpse of the wing—the screech of tires before that, the crunch and the pain—

None of that was here now. I tensed against the soft duvet that was cushioning my body but stayed still as I took in the room.

Blue wallpaper with a faint leaf pattern covered the walls. A big window stood across from the foot of the bed, closed, the gauzy curtains on either side drifting in a current that must have been thanks to an air conditioning system. A sheet was wrapped loosely around me, but the air against my face was cooler than made any sense for July.

If this even still was July. Who the hell knew with all the bizarre stuff I'd experienced in the last few hours... or days... or however long it'd been? Maybe I *had* gone dancing and someone had slipped me something awful that came with hallucinations?

But I was usually pretty careful about my drinks. And it wasn't like some wacko drug could explain what I was doing here, or where *here* was.

I pushed myself slowly into a sitting position. My pulse leapt for a second at the pull of the sheet against my shoulder, but the strange weight on my back was gone. I reached behind me to feel down my shoulder blade and found nothing but my regular bare skin. A breath rushed out of me.

Okay. So the wing, at least, has been a hallucination. Or something.

And the jeep hitting me? The agony and the bones I could swear I'd heard cracking?

I tested my arms and touched my ribs. Not even my skin was broken. Nothing hurt. Hell, I felt *better* than I did most days when I woke up, honestly.

There was also no sign of the row of tiny scabs I'd had on my wrist from a scuffle a week ago. I studied it, frowning. Maybe I had been out of it for longer than a day or two.

That idea made me edgy. My gaze fell on the clothes in a pile on the bed beside me. Preppy looking stuff, not what I'd have usually worn at all, but it beat going around naked. That part, and the sheet, had been real. The guys might very well be real too. Who knew when they might turn up again?

I pulled the clothes on quickly. The silky shirt was a bit baggy, but the pants fit without falling off my narrow hips, thank God. A light rose scent wafted off of them. That wasn't my usual style either, but I felt a hell of a lot better with that much less of my skin exposed.

What had happened to the clothes I'd been wearing when... when the jeep had hit me—or hadn't hit me—or whatever? What had happened to the things I'd been *carrying* in those clothes? My heartbeat stuttered again, and this time I couldn't find quick reassurance. I couldn't see anything in the room that belonged to me.

My fingers curled into my palms. My switchblade. I had to get it back. It was the only thing I had...

You hold onto this, and you use it if you have to, Ari. For the times when I can't be here.

I closed my eyes against the icy jolt and forced myself to breathe deep. In and out, until I felt a little steadier.

I'd get my knife back, and I'd deal with whoever had carted me off here. But first I needed to be prepared.

The view out the window showed me a three-story drop and a sprawling lawn with a border of trees. I couldn't see any neighbors, which meant it wasn't likely anyone out there could see me, and if I tried that jump—if the window would even open—I really would break all my bones.

Okay, so what did I have in here that I could use?

A glass of what looked like water and a plate with a Granny Smith apple and a stack of crackers sat on the bedside table. My eyes lingered on them. A pang crept up my throat, reminding me how dry my mouth was. My stomach was too tight with tension for me to want to put any food in it, though, even if I'd trusted this stuff. The people here could have put anything in it.

The bed's solid oak frame didn't offer much. Inside the matching massive wardrobe I found only more clothes, all in white and shades of gray.

The room had two doors—one, closed, beyond the enormous oak wardrobe, and another on the other side of the bed that was halfway open, revealing white tiles and the edge of a sink. I scooted across the bed and went into the bathroom.

My reflection in the mirror over the sink looked the same as usual. Maybe my gray eyes looked a little frantic, and the waves of my blond hair were particularly messy, but that was definitely still me: Aria Watson, twenty-two, short and scrappy and wingless.

I turned the tap and scooped a little water into my mouth with my hand. I trusted that stuff more than what was in the glass. Then I tried the mirror. It opened to a cabinet with a couple extra bars of soap, a dented tube of toothpaste, and a silver comb.

The comb's pointed handle looked like it could do some damage if used right. I grabbed the thing and tucked it into my right hip pocket.

A knock sounded on the other door, the one that must have led to the rest of the house. My shoulders stiffened. I drew the comb back out, wrapping my fingers around the teeth so I could stab with the pointy end if I needed to.

An elegant female voice carried through the door. "Hey in there. Would you mind if I came in? I'm thinking you must be rather confused. Any questions you have, I can do my best to answer."

A woman, not one of the men. The same woman I'd seen with them, who hadn't done a thing to help me? But then, maybe she hadn't had a choice with them around. Even if she was in on this scheme with them, I'd have a better chance of getting out of here if I figured out what was going on.

"Okay," I said tentatively. "But I definitely want those answers before anything else."

As I stepped back into the bedroom, the door eased open. It *was* the woman from before—the tall graceful figure with a cascade of honey-brown waves who looked as if she could have walked right out of a magazine fashion spread, Photoshopping still in place. Her perfectly fitted lilac sheath dress only amplified that impression.

She shut the door behind her and gave me a small smile that was a bit tight. Her gaze took in the comb clutched upside down in my hand, and one elegant eyebrow lifted.

"*That* isn't going to be necessary," she said.

"I'd like to take my time deciding that," I said. "And I'm staying over here. You can start explaining now."

She practically floated to the bed and set herself down gingerly on the edge, her body turned toward me. I backed up a step, but not too close to the wall. If it came down to a fight, I needed room to maneuver.

Not that this gal looked like much of a fighter. But you never knew. The prissy pretty ones could have cores of steel under all that polish.

"I'm sorry," she said. "The boys really made a hash of it, didn't they? You'd think after all the centuries they've lived, they'd have learned better manners."

All the centuries? "You're not really making things any less confusing," I said.

She inclined her head. "The most important fact is this: You died, and together we summoned your essence here and reformed you. With... a somewhat different constitution than you're used to. That's why you feel so strange. That's how you ended up here."

She stopped. I kept staring at her, waiting for her to follow that explanation up with something that sounded like part of reality, but apparently she was finished. Apparently *that* was supposed to explain everything.

A guffaw jolted out of me. "You're trying to tell me that you brought me back from the dead."

She looked back at me steadily. "It isn't that difficult a thing, when you're a god. Or a goddess, as the case may be."

Okay, I still didn't know how I'd gotten here or how the car crash I'd thought had ended me factored in, but clearly I was being held by a bunch of total psychotics. They thought they were *gods*? That couldn't be good. People deluded enough to think they were invincible were the most dangerous people out there.

But if I was going to get away from them, I'd have to play along for now.

"And what would a bunch of gods and goddesses want with me?" I asked.

The woman opened her mouth to answer, but at the

same time the bedroom door whisked open. I flinched, my hand tightening around the comb.

The figure in the doorway was one of the men I'd seen when I'd first woken up: Slim. Still tall and lean as before, his amber eyes as bright as his light red hair. The green tunic he was wearing made his hair gleam even starker.

He grinned at the two of us, the smirk as sharp as the angles of his handsome face, but his voice came out warm and smooth. "I don't think you should be doing all the talking here, Freya. I know you'll just make the rest of us look bad."

She rolled her eyes. "I think the rest of you did an excellent job of that with no help from me."

He made a scoffing sound and focused on me, with a little dip of his head that was almost a bow. "My apologies for your unsettling awakening earlier. Loki, at your service."

The woman's name hadn't quite connected, but I knew that one without even having to think. "Loki... like the Norse god who was supposed to destroy the whole world?"

His eyes gleamed even brighter. He sure looked the part, as crazy as he might be.

"I don't think I can take quite that much credit," he said. "It really was a joint effort."

I didn't know whether it was the stress of the situation or the ridiculousness—well, probably both—but all at once laughter bubbled up from my chest, too fast for me to catch it. I clutched my comb-weapon and pressed my other hand over my mouth, but the giggles spilled out anyway.

The guy who thought he was Loki looked at the woman who was supposedly Freya and said mildly, "You know, I don't think she believes us."

Then he snapped his fingers, and a burst of fire leapt from his hand, wide as his head and licking all the way up to the ceiling. A waft of heat cut through the air-conditioned room to brush my face.

I stopped laughing.

"Nice little trick, isn't it?" he said. With another snap of his fingers, the flames disappeared. His slender pale hand looked unmarked, but the fire had left a faint yellow-brown scorch mark on the white ceiling plaster.

Freya glanced up at it and wrinkled her nose. "Was that really necessary?"

"It seemed the quickest way to cut to the chase," he said. "So what do you think, pixie? Good enough, or do you need a little more? I could do a little shapeshifting ..."

He passed his hand in front of his face, and before my eyes his features shifted. His narrow jaw rounded, his angular features softened around the edges, and the pale red hair that had drifted over his high forehead spilled down to his shoulders in a cascade to rival Freya's. I'd swear even his eyelashes grew. In the space of a second, a lovely if shockingly tall woman was gazing back at me.

I blinked and blinked again. The bottom dropped out of my stomach. This was insane. Impossible.

But also way too real.

The guy... who maybe was the Loki from the myths I'd read as a kid? Was I really going to go there? He waved his hand, and his face fell back into its previous sharply handsome state. "Convinced yet?" he asked me.

"I, um..." My hold on the comb had faltered. I adjusted my grip, keeping my body rigid to stop myself from shaking. I didn't know what was true, but I couldn't deny whatever was going on here, it was deeply fucked up.

I wasn't going to get out of it unless I kept my head.

I pulled my posture a little straighter, glancing from Loki to Freya and back again. "I still want to know why either of you would have brought *me* here."

"Well, it's a bit of a long story," Loki said. "The gist of it is, we needed a valkyrie, and out of all the recently deceased young women in the area at the time we put out the call, you fit the profile the best. My profile, that is. The first few, we used different criteria, but those didn't work out all that well."

"A valkyrie," I repeated. He'd said that right before that other guy had knocked me out before. When I'd seen that wing...

The memory sent an uncomfortable shiver through my nerves.

"Yes, you know: Odin's champions, overseers of the battlefield, so on and so forth." He waved vaguely. "You see, we seem to have misplaced the Allfather, and having a valkyrie on hand ought to make tracking him down much easier."

I was already shaking my head. This was too much. "I don't know what you're talking about. I'm not a valkyrie, and I'm obviously not *dead*, and... This is crazy. Do you have any idea how crazy this is?"

"We brought you back," Loki said, so matter-of-factly it chilled me. "And we brought you back as a valkyrie. Quite a trick in itself. Your powers only manifest as you need them or call on them... It's easy enough to demonstrate."

He twitched his fingers, and a small knife appeared in his hand. Without missing a beat, he slashed it across his other palm. Blood welled up along the angry line, thick and a red so much darker than his hair. Freya grimaced and looked away.

And something stirred inside me.

My pulse thumped heavier, echoing through my head. A prickling raced through my muscles. Every nerve seemed to perk with a sudden awareness. The space between my shoulder blades quivered with a deepening itch.

"You can feel it, can't you?" Loki said. Both he and Freya were studying me now. "The call to battle. *Where blood is spilled, the valkyries fly.* All you have to do is open your wings."

"I—I don't have any wings," I said, but my voice sounded weak through the thumping of my heart.

He smiled. "Of course you do. You just have to let them out."

The itch on my back dug in even deeper. I sucked in a sharp breath. Wings. I couldn't have *wings*. Let them out? How—

In the back of my mind, without even meaning to, I pictured broad feathered wings like the one I'd caught a glimpse of before, spilling out from my skin. The itch between my shoulders burst with a jab of pain. Something —some part of *me* that I could feel echoing all through the rest of my body—stretched out against the thin fabric of the blouse, straining and unfurling and tearing right through.

I stumbled forward at the sudden weight and grabbed the bedframe to catch myself. The torn blouse hung from my chest, and from my back...

My throat tightened. I made myself glance back.

A huge wing, the feathers mingled white and pale silver, loomed over me.

My nerves jittered, and the wing twitched in response. Because my nerves ran through it too. Because it was part of me, just like the one I could feel weighing on the other side of my back.

I squeezed my eyes shut. The comb dropped from my fingers. "No. It can't—"

But it was. It was real. I could see them. I could *feel* them, not just on me but in me.

Loki's voice reached me, still smooth but gentler now. "You can send them away when you want to, too. They're yours. They follow your command. Just pull them back into yourself."

Yes. Get them away. Get them off of me. I clenched my teeth and willed that weight back into my body—let me absorb it, let them be *gone*.

The feel of the wings shrank until there was nothing left but a twinge on my back. Then that faded too. I opened my eyes with a gasp.

Freya had already opened the wardrobe. She pulled out another blouse, this one sleeveless and ivory, and offered it to me as she cut a glance toward Loki. "Let's try not to go through too many clothes all at once."

I accepted the shirt to replace the torn one drifting against my back. My fingers curled into the cool fabric. My hands were shaking. I bent to grab the comb off the floor, as if it could do much for me now.

Gods. Valkyries. And I was somehow mixed up in this all the way down to my bones.

I swallowed thickly and looked up at the god and goddess who'd just witnessed my transformation.

"Can you start over from the beginning? With the long version, this time."

4

Aria

As I stepped into the big room where I'd first woken up, I took in all the details I'd been too overwhelmed to notice before: the speckled gold pattern overlaid on the lighter yellow of the wallpaper, the two sofas and scattered armchairs with ornately carved teak frames. A bunch of lilies sat in a porcelain vase on one of the matching side tables, giving off a pungent perfume.

I never liked lilies. They made me think of funerals. At Francis's—

I cut off that thought before it could send me into the downward spiral of memory and meandered as if at random to one of the chairs. It wasn't really at random. I'd picked the chair closest to the far doorway. The one that, if I'd read the layout of this building well, should put me in the right direction to reach the front entrance.

The teeth of the comb bit into my palm as I sat on the

firm cushions. I kept my fingers wrapped tightly around it. The people who'd brought me here might not be people at all—might be actual gods, or something like it— but even if that was true, that didn't mean I was safe here. Or that I wanted to stick around.

Freya and Loki had called the others in the house to join us. The five of them settled into seats they'd pushed into in a semi-circle facing me, Loki in the middle. The man with the shaggy white-blond hair who'd knocked me out with his touch sat at his left, next to the guy who'd hung back during that first encounter.

The two of them were like a study in opposites but somehow eerily similar at the same time. The second guy had his black hair cropped short, and his dark green eyes were narrowed while his neighbor's bright blue ones drifted as dreamily as before. They were both a little shorter than Loki, with boyishly smooth faces and enough muscle to fill out their T-shirts, but the same features and build that looked soft on the dreamy guy had turned hard on the dark-haired one. He couldn't even be bothered to look right at me.

They were both striking-looking in their own ways, that was for sure. Apparently being a god meant divinely good looks. Which was true for the guy at Loki's right, too —the incredibly beefy guy with a dark auburn ponytail who'd tried to tame me with a sheet. When I looked at him, he gave me a smile that was slightly grim, but his broad, square-jawed face still couldn't have been easier on the eyes.

I had no idea who light-and-dark pair might be, but

given the company, I could make a stab at naming Mr. Muscles there.

"Let me guess," I said, pulling my legs up onto the chair—better if they thought I was getting comfortable. "You must be Thor."

The grim smile stretched into a wide grin. "Very good," he said in his mellow baritone. "You catch on quick. Do you mind telling us your name?"

They didn't know? I remembered what Loki said about me just fitting certain criteria. I guessed my name hadn't gone into that evaluation.

For a second, my chest clenched, as if my name was something I should hold onto. But I couldn't see how it really mattered. "Aria Watson," I said. "Ari, preferably."

"Nice to meet you, Ari," Thor said. For a god with a reputation for going around smashing things up with a giant hammer, he seemed pretty chill. The welcoming vibe he gave off made me start to relax despite myself.

My gaze darted back to the other side of the room. "And you two are...?"

"Allow me to introduce the opposite twins," Loki said with a flourish of his hand toward the pair. "Baldur and Hod."

"Hello," the dreamy pale guy said. His voice was melodic but kind of distant at the same time.

His dark... *twin?* shot a scowl Loki's way and then turned his narrowed eyes toward me. "Good to see you've settled down," he muttered.

Hod had some kind of stick up his ass, apparently. He couldn't really be blaming me for freaking out, could he? Or was he peeved I hadn't recognized them? Well, excuse me for not having read up on my Norse mythology in ten plus years. I'd had bigger things on my mind.

The name Baldur did sound kind of familiar, like he should be important. Hadn't there been some retro game Francis had raved about that was Baldur something? That probably had barely anything to do with the actual mythology... if the actual mythology even had anything to do with the supposed gods and goddess sitting across from me.

"So," I said, focusing back on Loki, since he seemed to be the biggest talker in the bunch. "You said you'd explain everything. What I'm doing here. What *you're* all doing here. From the beginning."

"Yes. Well." He smiled crookedly and ran a hand through his pale red hair. "You know who we are. How familiar are you with the stories that get told about us?"

"A bit," I said. "It came up in school when I was pretty little. I probably read some books from the library or something. But I'm no expert."

"All right. A relative blank slate." His amber eyes glinted. "The basic stories are mostly true. They also happened a long time ago. Since then we've been a lot less busy. So now and then, we pass the time by coming down to Earth and seeing what we can do for you lovely mortals."

"Or seeing what catastrophes you can create," Hod put in.

Loki ignored him. "We came down from Asgard—our home realm—on one of those ventures some time ago, the five of us here and Odin. Odin as in the Allfather, my blood-sworn brother, her husband"—he jabbed his thumb toward Freya—"and literal father to the rest of this lot. We're really the only ones who've kept together all that much. I'm not sure where in the nine realms Heimdall and Frigg and the rest of them are getting their itches scratched these days."

"Somewhere they don't have to listen to you blather on?" Thor suggested, but his voice was amused and the look he gave Loki almost fond. He turned to me. "The important part is, Odin has a thirst for knowledge that's never satisfied. He goes off on rambles all the time. So, he took off, and we didn't think anything of it. Until year after year passed without any sign of him."

Freya had folded her graceful hands in her lap. She looked up from them now. "He's been gone nearly twice as long as his longest 'ramble' before," she said.

I glanced from one to the next, trying to judge their reactions. "Okay," I said. "That sounds like reason to worry. But he's, like, a *god*, right? A pretty powerful one, if the stories are even mostly true. What kind of trouble could he have gotten into?"

Loki lifted his angular shoulder in a shrug. "There are beings of power in the realms other than gods. The Norns know even gods can turn on each other. And we aren't simply worried about him out of the goodness in our hearts, though we have plenty of that."

Hod snorted. Loki raised an eyebrow at him, but the sullen god didn't speak.

Baldur had looked toward his darker twin too. "Brother," he said in his lilting voice, gently chiding.

Hod's stance stiffened. He waved dismissively. "Go on, trickster."

EVA CHASE

So Loki did. "We're somewhat restricted in our powers while we exist on the mortal plane here in Midgard. The longer we remain here, the more those powers diminish. But Odin is the only one who can call up the bridge that will lead us back to Asgard. Once, there were paths to the land of the gods here and there from the other realms, but after Ragnarok he closed them all off."

"Got it," I said. "You need Odin back to let you all go home, because you don't feel godly enough here anymore."

Thor guffawed and clapped the arm of his chair. "There's one way of putting it."

Loki spread his hands as if to say, *What of it?*

I shifted in my seat. "But what the hell do you need *me* for? You're gods. What could anyone do that you can't?"

"Ah, you see, we do have a few gaps in our range of talents," Loki said. "And sadly, we never bothered to fit Odin with a tracking device. But we did discover that between the four of us with blood ties, we can bring about the valkyrie summoning. As a valkyrie, you have a different connection to Odin. In some ways a more direct one. And other special abilities that will serve the search well."

"So, I just have to find Odin and that's all there is to it?"

"We'll need to train you in your powers first," Thor said. "But they'll come naturally to you, so that won't take long."

"And what happens after I find him?" Could I just

34

waltz back into my regular life? Preferably without wings that wanted to sprout out of my back every time someone got a papercut around me?

"Let's not get ahead of ourselves yet," Loki said.

Oh, no, I wasn't letting them dodge that question. Or — "You've mentioned a couple times that there were other valkyries before me," I said. "If we've got this special connection to Odin, shouldn't they have found him already? What happened to them?"

Loki, Thor, and Freya exchanged a glance. Hod glowered at the floor, his mouth tense. Even Baldur's dreamy aura seemed to dim slightly.

"We're not totally sure," Thor said. "They went looking, and they haven't come back."

"Our best guess would be that they were caught up in whatever caught the Allfather as well," Loki said. "Which only lends proof to the possibility that he *is* caught and hasn't simply lost track of time. But you're better equipped than any of them were."

Hod muttered something and shook his head. Baldur cast another tender glance toward his brother, but his fingers flexed against the arms of his chair. "We must give it a chance," he said.

"Give *what* a chance?" I said, my fingers tightening around the comb. "What's so special about me?"

The corner of Loki's thin lips curled higher. "My companions here felt that an ideal valkyrie would be a young lady pure of heart and noble of deed. It's my opinion that pure-hearted noble-doers are also pushovers. Seeing as their approach wasn't working out, I suggested we look for someone more resourceful. Perhaps even cutthroat. Not afraid to get her hands dirty if survival required it. Wouldn't you say that you fit the bill?"

My shoulders tensed. How much did he know? Had he seen, somehow, exactly what I'd needed to survive?

Loki looked mildly back at me. They hadn't even known my name—that meant they didn't know any details, right? Just the gist of it?

I wet my lips. "I've survived a lot, if that's what you mean, yeah."

"Well, there you go. The others didn't have the smarts to fend for themselves properly. I can tell you'll do just fine."

"You've already admitted you don't know what happened to the other ones," I said. "So you have no idea what I'll even have to do. And I still want to know what happens if it is all fine and I get Odin back here for you."

Freya leaned forward. "I suppose you'd return to Asgard with us," she said. "Make a life for yourself there."

"I had a life here."

"As a mortal human," Loki said. "You're less mortal and not at all human now. That isn't your world anymore."

I bristled inside. He didn't get to decide that. It was the only world I'd ever had, even if it was often a shitty one. I had people there who needed me. I had to get back to Petey before too long.

But I could feel their intentions dragging on me as they looked back at me, like those wings had dragged on my back. They didn't care. They just wanted me to be their tool, for them to use to get what they wanted. What did they care what happened to me after? If I even made it through what the girls they'd summoned before me hadn't.

They could stick that plan where the sun didn't shine.

I tested my grip on the comb and the angle of my feet against the chair's cushion. "Let me think about it," I said.

Then I hurled myself over the arm of the chair toward the door.

5

Loki

She certainly was a slippery one, this new girl. One second sitting there casual as can be, the next leaping for the door as if Fenrir himself were at her heels. I had to admire her wits—and guts—even as I darted across the room to block her way. She was going to have to learn soon enough that she couldn't outrun us.

Our pixie skidded to a halt when I appeared in front of the door. Her gray eyes flashed. She swiveled in a blink and bolted for the nearest window, her tangled blond waves flying out around her shoulders.

I glanced toward Thor. He was already moving to intercept her. We made a good team when the situation called for it, despite our many differences.

But this girl—Aria, she'd said her name was—wasn't an enemy. We needed to subdue her *gently*. Without her getting hurt in the process.

She fumbled with the window, but the frame stuck. Thor reached for her. "Ari—"

She flung herself away from him, ducking under his massive arm and scrambling toward the other doorway. I might appreciate her perseverance, but this chase was getting a tad tiresome.

"Ari," I said calmly, my steps gliding across the floor several feet at a time. "Can I recommend less running, more talking?"

"There's nothing left to talk about," she said. She spun when I cut her off from the door and took off for the first door again.

All right, enough of this. "Hod," I said, clapping my hands. "Do us a favor and work a little of that wintery magic on our guest? It's difficult to have a conversation like this."

The dark twin glared in my general direction, but then his head turned as he followed the sound of the girl's footsteps. He swept his hand forward.

Ari jarred to a halt halfway across the room. She stared down at her legs, which had frozen in place amid a patch of conjured shadow. A frustrated sound burst from her lips. She looked around at all of us, her expression fierce. That damned comb was still clutched in her right hand, as if she could do the slightest bit of damage to any of us with that.

But this was what we'd asked for when we'd called into the void for a human spirit to shape into a valkyrie: a fighter. A survivor. Whatever she'd been through, no doubt she'd made it this far by *not* trusting anyone.

She was going to be perfect for this task, if I could just convince her to work with us instead of against us.

Her chin came up as I walked over to her. She stared back at me defiantly. "I don't want to be here. I don't want to be part of this... rescue operation, or whatever the fuck it is."

So much fire, even utterly helpless as she was now. I came to a stop a couple of feet away. A different person I might have extended a hand to, used touch to solidify the emotional connection I needed to make. But I'd seen how this girl reacted when anyone even got close to her. She'd been harmed by contact like that more than she'd been comforted.

I could adjust my usual strategies. A trickster was nothing if not adaptable.

Thor was lumbering over to join us. I waved him back, my gaze staying focused on Ari. A muscle in her jaw twitched, and she clenched it tighter. She was frightened under the defiance.

"Ari," I said, low and soft and most importantly, honest. "I understand. We've whisked you away from everything familiar, and now we're making demands and setting restrictions... Of course you don't want any part in that. *I* don't want to be doing this either. But it's the best idea we've come up with, and I swear we'll do whatever we can to ease your way—and it's better than being dead, isn't it? Because that was your alternative. The life you had is gone either way." I snapped my fingers. "Like that. Would you really rather you weren't here at all?"

Ari's shoulders started to come down. The angry flush faded from her face. She hadn't thought it through before, had she? We'd told her she'd died, but how could a mortal mind wrap itself around that possibility when as far as she could tell she was still perfectly alive?

"I was really dead?" she said. "Completely, not just... dy*ing*, or in a coma, or something?"

I nodded. "The magic we used to summon you could only latch on to a spirit already—if recently—detached from its former body. We rescued you from the void, pixie."

That muscle twitched again, but it wasn't fear this time. "I'm not a pixie," she spat out.

I let myself smile. "You haven't met any pixies if you take that as an insult. They're small, sure, but most of the ones I've known were tougher than I am."

With luck, she'd prove to be too. I needed her to be. The others had been hesitant enough about going along with my plan. If this situation went haywire, I wasn't going to convince them of anything else for another century or two.

If it went well, then maybe I'd get a little less grousing the next time I made a totally logical and insightful observation.

Ari didn't seem to know quite what to make of my response. She sucked her lower lip under her teeth. And abruptly I found myself noticing that along with being stubborn and bold and quick, she was rather pretty in her pixie-ish way. As if that observation helped us any at the moment.

"You're gods," she said finally. "Can't you do something about the whole dying thing? Bring me back to life as a human again?"

"Baldur might have, if he'd been there before you completely kicked the bucket," I said, nodding to the pale twin. "But he wasn't. And now that's done. We can't just flip a switch and send you back."

"So it's being dead or being trapped here."

"You're not exactly trapped," I said. "You'll have plenty of freedom—when we know you aren't going to run off and cause all sorts of chaos in the mortal world. We've given you a gift, really. We just want to be sure you're going to use it... responsibly."

She wrinkled her nose at me, but her gaze had turned thoughtful. Her jaw worked. And I made an educated stab in the dark. Cutthroat or not, almost every human had a soft spot for someone other than themselves.

"There are people back in that world you're worried about, aren't there?" I said. "People you care about? If you were dead, you really would be gone from their lives. Like this, you could at least keep watch from time to time. See them again. It might not be the same, but it's more than you'd have otherwise."

She was quiet for a moment, locked in that awkward stance with her legs mid-stride. "All right," she said. "I'll see what I can do to help you with this Odin thing if you'll teach me how to use these powers you gave me. And if you can get something for me."

Still making demands, huh? I managed not to chuckle, since she'd probably bristle at that. "What is it you want, pixie?"

She grimaced at the nickname, but not as sharply as before. "When I died, I was carrying some stuff on me. I had a switchblade in the right hip pocket of my jeans.

About four inches long folded, with a marbled dark blue handle. I want it back. *It* didn't die, so you can do that much, right?"

"I can," I said. It shouldn't even be that difficult, I didn't think. "I'll go get it right now. But I'll need to touch you. Hod, I think you can unfreeze her now."

She stiffened up even as Hod flicked his hand to dismiss the chilly shadow that had held her in place. But she stayed there, braced, as I shifted a little closer. Just close enough that I could rest my hand gently on the bare side of her shoulder.

The energy of her spirit tingled against my fingers. I absorbed the feel of it, the rush and the flow, the distinctive pattern that was hers alone. Then I stepped away from her and slipped out the door.

Outside, hot muggy air washed over me. I set off, letting the power imbued in my shoes of flight carry me. My strides stretched farther and farther until I was taking miles with every step—invisible to the mortal eyes I flew past, of course. On and on I soared through a blur of scenery until I'd traced the fading trail Ari's spirit had left to its source.

I came to a stop under the dim buzzing lights of a morgue. A rather unpleasant one even as morgues went. The air stunk with disinfectant and an underlying odor of rot, and the steel doors lined along one wall were smudged. I could tell which one our valkyrie's former body lay in; I could see in my mind's eye the mash of skull and brain and hair, the splintered bones. I didn't need to *really* see that.

Her belongings. They'd stripped off the clothes and

tossed them in a basket—here. And there was her precious switchblade. An interesting personal effect. I supposed it fit the girl.

I fished it out of the bloody fabric and washed it and my hands at the sink. The stench of death crept deeper into my lungs, and a shudder passed through me. Ugh. She had better give me plenty of credit for this.

I raced back the way I'd come, the knife nestled against my palm. When I strode back into our country house's living room, I found everyone arranged much as they had been in the beginning—Ari back in her chair, my godly companions scattered across the seats around her. No one was talking. They all appeared to have been waiting for me.

What a useless lot they were sometimes. I shook my head at them with a grin and held out my hand to Ari, brandishing the switchblade. Her face brightened. She snatched it from me and tucked it close to her chest.

Humans were such strange beings. I couldn't recall seeing a mortal that attached to a piece of weaponry since King Arthur and his legendary sword.

"There you have it," I said. "Do we have a deal?"

"I already said I'd try to help, didn't I?" she said, and paused. "There is something else that occurred to me."

I flopped back into my previous seat, stretching out my legs, only a tad winded from that lope across the country. "By all means, share your concerns."

She hesitated again. Then she said, "What would you do with me if I refused to follow your orders? If I told you to forget it, not a chance?"

Oh. She hadn't failed to think that aspect through. I

waited, but none of the others spoke up. Thor looked at his hands, folding them in front of him. They'd decided explaining this aspect was my job too. It figured, didn't it? Make Loki do the dirty work. That was how it always went.

I sighed. "We aren't cruel, Ari. We gave you this new life—we're not in any hurry to end it. If you decided you were going to do nothing more than sit around the house all day, then so be it. But we can't risk you endangering anyone else. You're our responsibility. If we felt you were making yourself a risk to mortal society—or anyone else—we would have to return you to the state in which we found you."

"Dead," she said, holding my gaze.

"Yes."

"I guess you haven't given me much choice then, have you?" she said, with a little smile so jagged it cut right through my chest.

I'd picked her. This was my doing. And now there was one more person who'd be pissed off if it turned out I'd been wrong.

6

Aria

For such a large house, the kitchen was awfully cozy. Just big enough for a countertop and the usual appliances—retro-looking enough that I suspected they were older than me, and possibly older than Mom on top of that—and a four-seater table tucked away in the corner.

I kind of liked it. I felt a lot more secure tucked away there, eating the sandwich I'd thrown together out of the wide assortment of options in the fridge and cupboard, than I would have at the vast dining table I'd caught a glimpse of on the way down the hall.

I'd planned to get started on this whole becoming super-powerful being right away, but the second I'd stood up again after my most recent escape attempt, a wave of dizziness had washed over me alongside a stomach gurgle loud enough that Loki had grinned. So I was going to stock up on energy and gather my strength before I took anything else on. I guessed it made sense that dying and being reborn and all that running around would have taken its toll.

Reborn as a *valkyrie*. My skin still crawled, remembering the alien weight of those wings. Could I actually fly with them? The idea made me shiver in a weird blend of anticipation and horror. My fingers squeezed around the handle of my switchblade, which I was still holding beneath the table. My borrowed slacks had pockets, but the warm plastic in my hand made me feel more grounded.

This whole situation was so crazy. Gods. Magic powers. Coming back from the dead. But I'd seen the proof with my own eyes. I *remembered* dying. I didn't know how anyone could have faked that or the stunts those gods had pulled. Those long minutes while my legs had been locked in place, prickling with the cold of the shadowy vise around them...

That was over now. No point in thinking about it. I had to focus on what was ahead. I'd learn whatever powers this weird collective could supposedly teach me, and then maybe I'd be in a position to slip their magical safeguards and actually get out of here.

From what I'd gathered, I'd lost less than a day. Petey wouldn't be worried about not seeing me or any gifts from me, not yet. Sometimes I'd had to go a whole week before I could safely drop in, and I'd just secreted him away for part of his lunch hour at the elementary school a few days ago.

Unless... What if the police had reported my death to Mom by now? What if she'd told Petey?

The image of his sweet and way-too-innocent little face swam up in my mind. The squeeze of his six-year-old's arms when he'd hugged me that last time. The excited sweep of his hands as he'd told me about the castle he'd built in class.

And also the holes forming at the toes of his shoes, because Mom couldn't bother to pick him up new ones. The shadow that had crossed his expression when he'd mentioned her and Ivan, her current guy.

You could keep watch, Loki had said. I was going to do a hell of a lot more than that. I could keep out of the rest of the "mortal" world—good riddance to most of it anyway—but I couldn't abandon my little brother. No way, no how.

I had to get back to him as soon as I could, just to let him know that I was okay—and that I'd never stop looking after him.

I took another bite of ham, lettuce, and mayo on rye, and Thor ambled into the kitchen. The gods had been giving me some space since our big talk, but I guessed his stomach had gotten the better of him too. He leaned over to peer into the fridge and pulled out a plate with a couple of leftover drumsticks, so big they had to be turkey or goose.

"Mind if I join you?" he asked.

I shrugged. "It's your house." Or was it? How exactly did real estate work when you were a divine immortal being?

In any case, it was more his than it was mine.

He sat down across from me and dug right into his meal, which as far as I could tell was a mid-morning "snack." In the time it took me to finish the last quarter of my sandwich, he'd cleaned one bone and pretty much finished the other, plowing through the meat with an occasional smack of his lips and a pleased gleam in his warm brown eyes.

"A body that big needs a lot of fuel to keep it running, huh?" I said.

Thor looked up from the bone he'd just inhaled one last fragment of meat off of. He blinked at me. Then a deep chuckle rolled from his lungs. "What can I say? Big guy, big appetite."

"Hmm," I said. "I could have polished two of those off."

He raised his eyebrows. "Oh, yeah?"

I jabbed my pointer finger at him. "Don't make any comments about me being a pixie or whatever either. I could drink you under the table too."

At that claim, he let out a full belly laugh, so powerful it rattled the table his legs had barely fit underneath. "Now *that* I would really like to see. I haven't even met another god who could out-drink me, unless it's Loki winning by trickery."

"Maybe later," I said, brushing the crumbs off my hands. "I'm thinking valkyrie lessons will probably sink in better if I'm sober."

"You can start with me if you'd like," he said. "Since I'm already here and all."

Out of my five saviors-slash-captors, I had to say Thor made me feel most at ease. Maybe because it seemed like there wasn't a whole lot of him that wasn't right there for me to see. He definitely didn't strike me as a schemer like Loki. And who knew what was going on in the heads of the others.

Thor, I got the impression, said what he meant, and if you didn't like it, well, maybe he'd convince you with that mythical hammer of his I figured had to be around here somewhere.

"All right," I said, getting up and sliding my switchblade into my pocket. "What part of valkyrie-ing are you an expert in?"

He chuckled again. "Come on. It's too hot to be running around outside, so we'd better use the great room."

The great room turned out to be a room even more vast than the living room we'd assembled in earlier. A huge brick fireplace dominated one wall, but the burnt logs in it looked old. An assortment of chairs, sofas, and tables had been pushed to the walls. Thor stepped into the middle of the empty space and wiped his hands together. I had the feeling he used this room for activities along the lines of what we were about to do fairly frequently.

"It was usually Odin who picked and created the valkyries," Thor said. "But we each have our own sort of connection to him and qualities we share that we were able to pass on to you." He gave me a broad smile. "I gave you lightning."

"Lightning?" I looked down at my arms. I hadn't felt all that zappy so far.

"Strong reflexes," he said. "Speed and power. You

were obviously pretty tough before, but now you are even more." He grinned.

"Hmm." I flexed my muscles. Did they have more juice than I was used to?

"Your powers will only fully activate when they're triggered—or if you consciously call on them," Thor said. "Otherwise we'd all go around smashing every glass we picked up and stomping holes in the floor accidentally."

I cocked my head at him. "Somehow I think you're speaking from personal experience there."

He laughed. "Maybe. Let's just say it's useful to be somewhat normal when normal is all you need. But I can help you get a sense of the strength you can call on, so you know how to reach for it. I'll just need to provoke it a little..."

He took a sudden step toward me and swung his fist at my head. My pulse jumped, and I ducked. He hadn't punched that hard, I could tell from the breeze of his arm passing over my head, but he wasn't going completely easy on me. His other fist was flying toward me an instant later.

I scrambled backward across the smooth hardwood floor, and Thor followed. He was still smiling, but the glint in his eyes was so eager it was almost terrifying. He *could* pummel me into a pulp if he wanted to—I had no doubt about that.

The thought sent a jolt of panic through my chest that seemed to splinter there, tingling through all my nerves. I wove and dodged, but each movement smoothed out, coming faster and easier. The frantic beat of my heart settled into a sharp but steady drumming. I slipped out of Thor's range with a speed that took my breath away.

Lightning. That was what this felt like, all right. Electricity dancing through my veins.

"You can feel it now, can't you?" Thor said, sounding not even slightly out of breath. This whole exercise was no effort for him at all. "Get a little creative. Play around with it. You can do more than you might think."

He ducked his head in an unexpected charge, and I leapt out of the way. The push of my legs propelled me up over him. I found myself spinning past him and landing with a thump in a crouch behind him. The impact barely rattled my bones. A startled laugh spilled from my lips.

I was a fucking superhero now. Just try to let anyone stop me when I got the hang of this upgraded body.

Thor upped his game now that I was finding my feet. He moved faster, swung harder, and tried to trip me up with slashes of his feet as well as his fists. I kept darting out of the way even more quickly, the air whistling in my ears.

We circled the room at least a dozen times. I rebounded off the walls, vaulted from the furniture. Each move came even more effortlessly.

A prickling burn was spreading through my muscles, but it was a *good* burn. Like I was pushing them to a limit they'd always wanted to reach. I didn't know how long we'd been at this, but I felt like I could keep going for hours.

An impulse gripped me to push *him* harder. Why did I have to be always on the defensive here? Anyone smart knew you didn't go starting fights you didn't need to get into—but they also knew to go for the gut if the fight came to you.

I dodged another punch and sprang forward instead of backward. My fist swiped at Thor's well-packed belly. His arm slammed down to block me. My knuckles smacked his gut for just an instant before his block sent me tumbling to the side.

My enhanced reflexes kept me on my feet, just barely. The side of my arm throbbed just above my elbow where he'd hit me. I dropped into a crouch, holding that arm carefully, ready for him to come at me again.

But Thor's hands had dropped to his sides. He did come, but it was carefully, his mouth twisted with concern. His voice was ragged.

"Shit. I didn't mean to— You surprised me, and I couldn't catch my reaction in time. Are you all right?"

It was weird seeing the man who'd been so joyfully throwing punches at me a moment ago suddenly so subdued and worried. I straightened up, offering my arm for him to inspect. "You didn't get me that hard. It'll probably bruise, but I'll live."

He touched my arm gingerly, eyeing the red blotch where his block had made contact. "I could ask Baldur to heal it. I shouldn't have hurt you at all."

His obvious sense of guilt sent a twinge through me. When had *anyone* in my life ever been this concerned about how they might have hurt me? And he hadn't even, not really.

I forced my voice out, keeping it as casual as I could, with a wry smile for good measure. "It's fine. My fault for taking you by surprise. The bruise will be a reminder that next time I try, I just need to be faster."

Thor peered into my eyes as if making sure I was serious. His stance relaxed. He threw back his head with a laugh. "You are something, Aria Watson. There aren't many gods who could have landed a punch at me, you know? I guess I'd better watch myself."

He met my eyes again with a warm grin and a glint in his gaze as if he really were impressed. Impressed with *me*. He'd kept a little distance between us, but he was close enough that I could feel the warmth of his whole body. Smell him, tangy and heady like some fine, ancient liquor. What the hell did Norse gods drink? Mead?

Thor's broad hand was still cupping my elbow, his fingers curled gently against my bare skin. My sense of that touch quivered up my arm and down low in my belly. All at once I found myself wondering whether his skin would taste like he smelled. What it would be like to be touched like that, while he looked at me like that, in all sorts of other places.

The clearing of a throat on the other side of the room broke the moment. I jerked away from Thor and spun around to see Freya standing by the doorway. Her expression was amused.

"Managed to bash her up already, did you?" she said. "We've been hearing you thundering around for over an hour. Maybe it's time for a little break, or we'll wear our valkyrie right out." Her gaze focused on me. "What do you say to a little stroll while you catch your breath?"

Ah, yeah, a little breath catching sounded about right.

Because no way should I have been entertaining the thoughts I'd just had, not even for a second.

"I'll finish beating you up later," I told Thor, and tried to ignore the eager leap of my pulse as his chuckle followed me out the door.

7

Aria

When Freya had said a little stroll, she meant outside the house. The stark sunlight should have washed out someone with a fair complexion like hers, but it just made her hair shine like pale bronze and highlighted the rosy flush in her cheeks. I couldn't remember a whole lot about her from my childhood reading, but I was going to go out on a limb here and say whatever she was the goddess of, beauty had to be on the list somewhere.

I guessed she hadn't had a big role to play in summoning me here, seeing as valkyrie-me looked the same all-right-but-hardly-spectacular as the regular me had.

A narrow path where the bare dirt was packed hard cut across the lawn and into a stretch of meadows between scattered trees. Freya's white sandals skimmed over the ground, making barely a sound compared to the tap of my sneakers. Other than the breeze rustling the trees and lifting the summer heat a bit, that was the only noise around us. I still hadn't made out any neighboring buildings.

"Where are we, anyway?" I asked, right before an unnerving idea hit me. "Are we still on the... the 'mortal plane' or whatever you guys call it?"

A smile curved Freya's lips. "Yes, this is Midgard," she said. "We *can't* leave, at least not back to Asgard, without Odin. We're in the Hudson Valley, not too far from New York City. Some of the boys like to soak in the big city atmosphere while we're here."

I wasn't sure what "not too far" meant in godly terms, but I couldn't be all that far from home then. Once I got away from here, the question would just be how to get to someplace with proper transportation to get me the rest of the way to Philly.

The big brick house was hidden by the trees now. If I made a run for it here, Loki and the others wouldn't be around to stop me. Of course, I didn't know what powers Freya might have. And I didn't even know what direction I'd want to run in.

Just bolting hadn't worked out so well for me before. I was going to be smarter about my escape next time. Think it through. Be prepared for anything.

Freya glanced over at me. "Is that where you were living? New York?"

I blinked at her. They really didn't know much about me, did they? "No," I said. "Philadelphia. I've been to the Big Apple a couple times, but... I like Philly better." More compact. Less snooty, at least if you didn't go too far out into the suburbs. And familiar as the back of my hand.

Freya hummed to herself. "I'm sure we've been through there at least once or twice. At this point, we've been through pretty much everywhere." She laughed briefly. "And you have family there? Friends?"

"Some." Not any that really mattered other than Petey. Not any I wanted to talk to her about.

"And what exactly did you occupy yourself with out there that made Loki think you were the type to get your hands dirty?"

Her expression had turned a little sly. Of course this "stroll" wasn't just to give me a break in my training. She wanted something from me too. To know just how big a mess the girl they'd picked up almost at random was. My hackles rose, but I kept my voice calm.

"I left home when I was seventeen. Been looking after myself for the last five years. When you're starting with nothing, you do what you have to. I work for criminals. I've bent the law. I've stolen when it was either that or starve—or when I saw someone who really didn't deserve what they had. I've hurt people when it was either that or get hurt."

Because I hadn't done enough of that when it really would have made a difference. A painful jab ran through my gut.

"A survivor," Freya said.

I didn't like her flippant tone. What the hell would a goddess know about needing to survive?

"More than that," I said. "I was doing pretty well, the last few years. I've got an apartment that's all mine, no roommates needed. Clients I can count on as far as anyone can count on a criminal. It was a life." I wasn't going to tell her about Petey.

"But one of these criminals killed you?"

"No," I muttered, kicking at a stray pebble. My lightning-forged muscles sent it flying straight across the meadow. "Some asshole junkie in a jeep killed me."

"Ah." Her brow furrowed. "I may have experienced plenty of the modern age, but I do still find humankind's motorized vehicles rather disturbing."

"Well, they're particularly 'disturbing' when they're bearing down on you at a hundred miles an hour." I hoped that idiot driver had gotten bashed up bad in the crash. Lost his license. Some sort of karma.

Freya switched gears on me. "Seventeen is rather young to be leaving your home, isn't it?"

"Yes," I said stiffly. "But I had good reasons." Reasons I *definitely* wasn't getting into with her. Echoes of shouting and funerals and the ghost of unwanted hands traveling over my skin washed over me just with that quick mention. I shoved all those memories way, way back in my mind where they belonged and hopefully would stay for the rest of eternity.

I was going to save Petey from all that—from all the shit I'd been through under Mom's roof.

Restlessness rippled through me. I found myself looking into the distance again. Wondering how far in the distance I could find a real road where I might be able to hitch a ride before anyone caught up with me. Yeah, right.

When I yanked my gaze back, Freya was watching

me with a tense little smile. A prickle ran down my back. Did she know what I'd been thinking?

Maybe she'd brought me on this walk out here just to test me—to see whether I'd try to run again. To make sure I really was committed now.

But look, here I still was. She couldn't complain about that. Now maybe she'd cough up a little more information about this bizarre little family of hers. The better I understood where they stood with each other, the easier I'd be able to work my way out of this crazy situation.

"So you're Odin's wife," I said. "And the other gods... are his sons?"

"Other than Loki," she said with an arch of her eyebrow. "He's no relation to any of them, as much as he might enjoy playing otherwise. He and Odin swore an oath to each other, a very long time ago. We've been stuck with him since then."

"Blood brothers," I said, remembering how Loki had put it.

"Yes. Thor and the twins are Odin's sons, from before our partnering." She exhaled softly. "Many things have changed in our realm since the days when humankind honored us."

Hold on. "Baldur and Hod really are twins?" I said. "I thought Loki was making a joke."

She laughed. "Understandable, but no. Non-identical, clearly, but born together all the same. Day and night. Summer and winter. And yet inseparable, other than..." Her voice trailed off, and she shut her mouth.

"Other than?" I prompted.

"Nothing. I lost my train of thought." She waved dismissively.

Ah ha. There were things the gods didn't want to talk about too. But I couldn't see pressing directly getting me any further.

"They get along, then?" I said. "Hod struck me as a little, um, grouchy."

Freya's smile came back. "He is that. But their bond is something else. And as their older brother Thor naturally keeps an eye on both of them, never mind they've been grown adults for innumerable years."

A close-knit family. Loki on the outside, but he was also clearly the sharpest of the bunch, so I couldn't see him as a weak spot.

Our path had taken us in a wavering circle. The house came back into view up ahead, the old bricks dark against the bright green foliage all around them. If I couldn't find a weak point among the gods, maybe their home had one. From this angle I could see the front and back porches and windows rambling all up the side I was facing. A couple of those were close enough to jump from... Even the third-floor ones might work if I could use these wings to fly. My back itched at the idea.

I didn't like the feel of them, but if that was what it took, I'd do it. I just needed to learn how first. I'd find out what the other three gods had to teach me, and then I'd be ready.

"Thank you for the walk," I said, tucking my hair back behind my ears as we reached the front of the house. "I think it was good to clear my head. Now I guess I'd better get on with this training I'm supposed to do."

"Thank you for the company," Freya said smoothly, as if she hadn't been using it as an excuse to pump me for information and who knew what else.

When we stepped inside, a lilting melody was carrying faintly down the stairs. Like a violin, maybe, but lower. And vaguely familiar.

Freya tipped her chin toward the stairs. "That'll be Baldur. You could go see him next."

Baldur. The dreamy bright god who'd knocked me unconscious with his touch—but in about as peaceful a way as anyone could ask for. I wasn't sure what to make of Loki yet, and Hod definitely didn't like me. I might as well find out what was going on behind those slightly dazed if gorgeous eyes, and what he'd contributed to my valkyrie-ness.

The song petered out as I reached the top of the stairs. Whatever piece it had been, the one he started playing next was even more familiar: the swelling notes of "Amazing Grace." I'd taken singing classes for a little while when I was a kid during one of Mom's rare generous phases. I'd sung that piece for my first and only recital.

The lyrics tickled at the base of my throat as I came up on the closed door the music was seeping through. As I eased it open, I couldn't help letting my voice slip out softly in time with the instrument.

"Through many dangers, toils and snare, we have already come. T'was grace that brought us safe thus far, and grace will lead us home."

Hell yes, I could use some of that kind of grace right now.

8

Baldur

The bow moved over the strings as smoothly as if it had a mind of its own—as if it were playing the music of its own accord, and my hand was simply coasting along with it. The low rich notes of the viola filled the room. I wasn't even paying attention to what song I moved to next, just letting instinct carry me. Losing myself in that world made of warmth and music. The only world where everything always felt perfectly at peace.

A voice wove through the melody. Raw but sweet, wavering on a note here or there but mostly hitting just the right cadence. My eyes popped open.

The young woman who was our new valkyrie had just slipped into the room. She froze, her mouth snapping shut, when my gaze met hers. I eased the bow to a stop.

"You have a good voice. It seems your parents named you well."

Aria's mouth twitched. She looked as though she wasn't sure whether she should smile. "My voice isn't half as good as you play," she said. "Is it normal for Norse gods to learn Christian hymns?"

"Is that what that song was? I have to admit I don't always take note of the source. I hear music I like, and I store it away up here." I tapped my head lightly.

"You must have quite a collection now."

After all the time of my existence, she meant. A quiver ran through my thoughts. I looked away, breathing in, settling into the warm glow the song had left behind that matched the sunlight streaming through the window of the music room. There was nothing distressing here. And the past wasn't worth thinking about, now that it was past.

When I turned back to Aria, she was watching me warily. "I didn't mean to interrupt," she said. "I thought maybe you could start your part of the whole valkyrie training thing."

"Of course," I said. Good that she was willing; good that she was eager. I smiled. "You want to understand what you are now as much as possible. I'll help in every way I can."

I stood up and set the viola in its place against the wall amid our collection of instruments. I'd dabbled in a variety over the eras, but the viola was one I kept coming back to. Nothing else could quite match the depth and purity of its sound. I trailed my fingers over the smooth wood affectionately.

"What exactly is it that you're going to teach me?" Aria said. "I'm still not totally sure how you all fit in."

I nodded. Some confusion was understandable, but I should do what I could to soothe it. My gaze slid back to her. "It will take time to absorb everything. I'm sorry your arrival was so difficult for you. We've tried to welcome our valkyries as gently as possible, but it's such a complicated situation. If there had been a way, I'd have wanted your permission first."

She did smile back then, a little wryly. "Well, it's done now, right? And I can't say I'd rather I was back to being dead. So I guess it worked out okay."

She *was* different from the other ones. I hadn't been sure of Loki's reasoning when he'd made his case for a new strategy, but I could see the benefit of it in her now. The others—they'd agreed to help out of the goodness of their hearts, which they'd had plenty of. It'd been goodness they'd turned to when their fears or uncertainties had crept up. But goodness was soft and hazy.

The determination in Aria was something flexible but so much stronger, like the robust tension of a good bow. She wanted to learn because it was a challenge she looked forward to defeating, not just because she felt obligated to follow some vague idea of rightness. She was going to *enjoy* coming into her powers, not simply accept them as a duty.

That kind of light could sustain you so much longer, through so much more.

She'd bounced back quickly from the frantic girl she'd been this morning. It soothed *me*, seeing that.

"What do you know about valkyries?" I asked her.

"Other than what you guys have told me so far—that they've got something to do with Odin, and you've got to use someone dead to make one?" She shrugged. "Not much. They're warriors, right? That's why I needed some of Thor's strength in the mix?"

"In a way," I said. "But a valkyrie's position is something more sacred than that. In the old times, you and your sisters would have watched over the battles on Midgard and decided which side emerged victorious. Chosen which of the fallen deserved to ascend to Odin's great hall, Valhalla. Justice and mercy."

Her eyebrows lifted. "Sounds like a big responsibility."

There really wasn't much that fazed this one, was there? I felt myself relax even more into the conversation. I was giving her something she wanted. There was no discomfort here.

"Yes," I said. "Although you wouldn't have shouldered it alone. There would have been dozens of you, observing and considering."

"But now you're stuck with just me. After the trouble the ones before me apparently had, you didn't think a squadron might be a good idea?"

"Ah," I said, with a wave of my hand as if I could brush both of us past that point. "It takes a lot of energy for us to summon even one valkyrie. We do the best we can. Now, I can show you—"

"What happened to the other ones?" Aria broke in.

I cocked my head. "The previous three we

summoned disappeared in their search. Loki mentioned that, didn't he?"

She folded her wiry arms over her chest. "I don't mean the ones you summoned. I mean all those dozens of valkyries Odin had before, off in Valhalla or wherever. If they're so attuned to him, why aren't they already looking? Why'd you need to make your own?"

Before. Another quiver ran through my consciousness, but only along the surface. Easier to sweep aside.

"It's been a long time since those days," I said. "Things have changed. Your wars have gotten so much larger. The old ways no longer made sense. Odin released the valkyries from their duties and the powers that came with them."

"Oh. That sucks all around, doesn't it?" Aria dragged in a breath. "All right. So what's next, teacher? How do justice and mercy fit in for me?"

Yes, back to the real matter at hand. "When making their judgments, valkyries needed to see inside the warriors they were judging," I said. "To sense their motives and emotions. Like shining a light on their souls."

"Got it," she said. "And you're the god of light."

Another smile stretched across my face. Yes. We all had our place—and she was finding her place among us already, wasn't she?

"Something like that," I said. "And you have that ability too. If you learn the right focus, you can sense what others are feeling—the harmony or lack thereof in their spirit—even from a distance."

"Like over a battlefield."

"Exactly. Although we hope it won't come to that. But it should help you, if you encounter anyone during your search for Odin, to decide whether they're a threat or a potential ally."

I glanced around, considering how we might best practice this skill, and the sound of a car engine drifted in from outside. I couldn't have asked for better timing. Beckoning Aria to follow me, I walked over to the window.

A small truck had just pulled up at the end of our drive. A young man hopped out of the back with a cooler and a couple of boxes of groceries. A middle-aged woman climbed out of the front passenger seat and hauled out a bag of gardening equipment. The gray-haired man who'd been driving followed the younger man over to the house.

"Our mortal maintenance crew," I said to Aria as she joined me. She peered down through the glass. "They bring supplies from town and keep up the property so we don't need to worry much about it ourselves."

"You're not worried they'll see something godly?" Aria asked.

"Loki makes sure they see nothing that would disturb them."

She made a skeptical sound. "I get the impression he'd probably have fun disturbing them, really."

I had to laugh at that. "You might be right. But he manages to keep that part of his nature in check. We all want to keep the harmony here."

"Especially when you don't know how much longer it'll be before you can get home."

She knew how to cut straight through to the heart of

the matter too, didn't she? I closed my eyes for a moment, soaking in the sunlight and the familiar scents of the instruments and old paper scores.

"Yes," I said. "There's that. But it won't hurt them at all for you to try your sensitivity on them. Watch the woman from here, see if you can reach out to her with your mind. Almost as if you're going to caress her head with your thoughts. See what impressions come back to you then."

Aria leaned toward the windowpane, the errant blond waves of her hair nearly brushing the glass. Her eyes narrowed.

As she focused on the gardener, I found myself focusing more intently on our valkyrie. On the rise and fall of her chest, so close to mine, as her breaths evened out in concentration. On the light that lit in those gray eyes, the smile that started to curl her lips, when she must have caught what she was looking for.

I could get my own sense of *her* emotions, looking at her. There was that determination I hadn't needed any godly power at all to read. Beneath it, a growing sense of satisfaction—with the abilities she was discovering, I assumed. She wasn't *happy* here exactly, but I didn't think we could have expected that much yet. Content was a victory in itself.

And then, even deeper beneath that, I tasted a small but vivid pulse of love. Someone or something she held in her heart, so tightly and fiercely I had the urge to unravel it, to delve into every crinkle of that sensation. When was the last time I'd immersed myself in an emotion that strong? My pulse stuttered, half eager, half fearful.

Aria turned her head, and I jerked my awareness back to the surface. Her eyes were outright glinting now.

"I could feel it," she said. "When I reached out, like you said. Not a lot, but— She's a little worried. I think she has a pet at home that's sick. But she likes being out in the sun, working with her hands, seeing that the plants are growing well. She wants to do a good job even though she knows she's not being supervised closely."

Aria grinned at me triumphantly when she finished. I hadn't reached out to the gardener myself to compare my impressions, but everything she'd said felt right with what I knew of the woman.

I nodded encouragingly. "Try our delivery boy next, then."

I pointed to the young man who'd clambered back into the bed of the truck. He was sorting through a few boxes still sitting there, the sun bringing out a sheen in his dark brown hair. Aria leaned forward again, watching him. This time she spoke as she reached her awareness.

"He wishes he was back home," she said in a distant voice, with me and also with him. "There was something happening in town today that he's missing, and he's kind of peeved about that. But he's also intimidated by the house. He wants to make sure he hasn't forgotten anything he was supposed to bring in—so he doesn't get in trouble, I guess?" She glanced at me, coming back. "Has he gotten in trouble before?"

"Not that I can recall," I said. "As I mentioned, we try to keep harmony around here. No ill feelings. But mortal emotions aren't very often rational."

"Whereas godly emotions are?" Aria said, sounding

amused. She peered up at me. "And what would I see if I reached out to *you*, god of light?"

I felt her attention on me like the flicker of heat from a flame. Seeping through the calm glow on the surface down toward a deeper space where things I didn't want to look at closely started to stir in response.

My chest hitched. I stepped to the side, breaking her focus. "I think you've proven you've caught on fast," I said. "Maybe we can find a crowd to test those abilities out on next time. You're already well on your way."

Her brow knit as her gaze followed me, but she didn't push the matter. She did turn back to the window. "A little more practice couldn't hurt, right?" she said. "I wonder what's going on in that other guy's head."

As she bent forward, I stayed where I was, the brief jitter of my nerves settling with that distance.

This one was different, all right. Maybe in some ways I'd rather she wasn't.

9

_____

Aria

I left the music room with a weird twist in my gut. I'd learned what I needed to from Baldur. He'd been nice enough about it. But I couldn't shake the feeling that something had shifted while I'd been with him, something that had made his enthusiasm for the whole teaching thing dry up. He'd wanted me to leave at the end.

It shouldn't have mattered to me. I just couldn't help wondering what mystery lay behind those dreamy blue eyes. Because there was *something* more to him than rainbows and sunlight.

Curiosity killed the cat. Keep your eyes on the prize. Sayings I should keep in mind. Whatever was going on with any of these guys—gods—it had nothing to do with me.

I'd only taken two steps down the hall when Loki

peeled himself off the wall he'd been leaning against near the staircase. "I take it you've been making the rounds," he said in his smooth wry voice.

"That's what I'm supposed to be doing, right?" I said. "Getting up to speed on this valkyrie gig, so I can find your missing Allfather?"

The slim god grinned. "And with such enthusiasm. I'm just offended you haven't shown any interest in seeing what I can teach you yet. Unless you were simply saving the best for last."

He didn't sound offended even a little bit. I rolled my eyes. "You just weren't conveniently available."

"Here I am now." He spread his arms as if offering himself. "Shall we?"

I didn't like showing any weakness, but I hesitated despite myself. Loki was a trickster. The other gods even called him that. I might have held my own with some of the toughest criminals in Philly, but none of them had divine cleverness on their side. Not to mention it was his fault more than any of the others I was stuck here.

And on top of that, now that I wasn't in escape mode, it was hard not to notice just how freakishly attractive all of the gods were. With the others, I could distract myself. But Loki—quick-tongued and full of sly humor along with the power that practically radiated from that leanly muscled frame—was exactly my type. Exactly the type I'd have steered clear of to jump some other guy's bones when I had that itch, because I only wanted someone I could forget about the next day.

Loki was doubly dangerous just because of the urge that lit up in me at the spark in his eyes—the urge to

surprise him, to impress him, to beat him at his games...
and we wouldn't get into all the things certain parts of me
would have liked to do after that.

But I didn't really have a whole lot of choice about
spending time around him, so I'd just have to keep
reminding myself of the whole evil trickster god angle.

While I was coming to that conclusion, Loki's
expression softened, which somehow managed to make
his angular face even more attractive.

"Perhaps we didn't get off on the best of feet," he said,
his tone turning self-deprecating. "My fault, mainly, as so
much always is. Are there any other cutting instruments I
can retrieve to help make it up to you?"

I looked at him, a bit of the focus Baldur had taught
me tingling at the back of my skull. It was harder getting a
read on a god than a mortal. I'd barely felt anything from
Baldur before he'd broken the connection. Loki gave me a
faint impression that was fiery and yet cool at the same
time—and a sense of genuine apology. I was pretty sure
he *would* have gone running back to Philly to grab a
butter knife out of my kitchen drawer or the scissors from
Mom's bathroom cabinet if I'd asked him to.

I was kind of tempted to make him do it, just for the
hell of it. But what if that made me more indebted to
him? Nope, safer to stick to the essentials.

"I think I'm good in the cutting department," I said.
"If you're ready to teach, then teach. What valkyrie skills
have you got up your sleeve?"

The sly light in his amber eyes flickered brighter. "All
the best ones, pixie. Come with me. I'm going to teach
you how to fly."

A shiver of excitement raced through my chest as I followed him to the end of the hall. I was going to *fly*, like a fucking bird. But the excitement came with a knot in my stomach at the thought of calling those heavy wings out of my back.

Loki popped open the dormer window there and eased it up high enough for us to climb out onto the roof. Hot air and the tarry smell of baking shingles wafted through the opening. He swept his arm with a hint of a bow to let me go ahead of him. "Ladies first."

"I wouldn't say I'm a 'lady,'" I said. "But I'll take it anyway."

I clambered out onto the slanted roof, setting my feet carefully as I found my balance. The warm breeze licked through my hair. We were three stories up, with a view over the lawn and the tree-lined meadows. The sun was dropping low in the sky, making the trees' shadows stretch across the grass.

That was a long drop below us if I lost my footing. But maybe valkyries didn't break that easily. I wasn't especially keen to find out.

Loki slipped through the opening as if his much taller body fit as well as mine had, with a casual, confident grace. I jerked my gaze away before I started admiring him or anything stupid like that and looked out over the lawn. The maintenance people had driven off in their truck a few minutes ago. No one else around. Quite the pocket of privacy the gods had found here.

"So, I guess if I'm going to fly I'll need those wings." I rolled my shoulders, the sleeveless shirt Freya had picked out for me shifting with them. It had a racerback, leaving my shoulder blades bare. I might be able to unfurl my new appendages without ruining any more clothing.

My back had already stiffened at the thought of encouraging my wings to emerge. The last time I'd already been stirred up by the sight of Loki's blood. Now I had to totally calmly just *decide* to do it.

Loki was studying me. "You don't like them," he said.

It was hard to argue when he put it that plainly. "Nope," I said. "Not exactly the most comfortable feeling, having two strange—and huge... things sprouting out of your body that aren't supposed to be there."

"You're thinking about it wrong," he said, leaning his elbow onto the top of the dormer. "I can take on forms with all sorts of bits and pieces I'm not used to: wings, tails, hooves, breasts." He arched his eyebrows. "But I don't see them as foreign parts I'm stuck with. They're more like different facets of my own body that I'm bringing to the surface. And that's what your wings are. They *are* meant to be there now. They're yours. Own them. Embrace them."

I dragged in a breath. Maybe he had a point. I was going to have to get used to the wings if I was going to *use* them—to get out of here, to get to Petey, and to get through who knew what else lay ahead of me. The thought of them lurking under my skin still made me feel itchy, though.

"Bring them out slowly," Loki suggested. "Take your time absorbing the feeling, getting to know them. I can help you adjust your stance so you can hold them more easily."

He stepped toward me, and my body tensed at the

sudden movement. His hand paused half a foot from my shoulder. Again, he seemed to study me.

"If it's all right with you that I help?" he said.

I swallowed thickly. While the trickster god might not have Baldur's ability to read emotions, he clearly didn't miss much. The thought that he might be able to guess the deeper sources of my discomfort made the itch turn into an uneasy prickling. But this was why he was here. To teach. To help me figure out this valkyrie thing.

People who just wanted to shove you around—or worse—didn't generally ask for permission first.

"Okay," I said. "Slow and steady. Let's do this."

Loki let just his fingertips rest on my back where my wings would emerge, his touch so light I barely felt it. "Picture them, as you did before," he said softly. "Easing out from inside you, stretching up bit by bit..."

I needed those wings. I needed to fly. I took another deep breath and brought up the memory of the wings emerging. The itch dug into my back. Dug in and closed around the ridges of cartilage waiting to burst out.

Yes. Out you come. Easy now.

I nudged them with my mind, a push and a tug. A burning sensation trickled across my shoulder blades. Then they were rising, spreading over me, inch by feathered inch, their weight pressing down on me more with each passing second.

"There," Loki murmured. "These are yours—just as much as those pixie arms and legs are. Your muscles. Your bones. Your nerves. Straighten your back, here." He pressed my spine. "And round your shoulders just slightly—yes."

As I adjusted my stance to his instructions, the weight of the wings melted across my back. Still there, but not quite as intrusive.

"Flex them," he said, stepping back to give me room. "Try them out, just standing here. Feel how much a part of you they are."

I focused on the wings, and they responded. They unfurled wider over me with a sensation as if I were stretching my arms over my head.

My muscles. My nerves.

I curled the tips in again with a tentative flap, and the feathers stirred the breeze. The movement of the air tingled down through the wings. It quivered right through the rest of my body in a way that wasn't exactly unpleasant.

My wings. *Mine.* And they were going to take me home.

"So how do we get from this to flying?" I asked.

Loki grinned. "At some point you just have to take a leap."

He sprang into the air—and stayed there, hovering just beyond the edge of the roof. I eyed him.

"How do you do that?"

"Magic!" he said with a snap of his fingers, and chuckled. "Somewhat literally. I happen to be in a possession of a pair of highly supernaturally charged shoes."

"Hmm. Maybe I could just borrow those."

"You could try. Unfortunately for you, they're tuned only to work on my feet. Of course, you could simply make use of those glorious wings of yours already. Come on." His tone turned into a challenge. "Bet you can't catch me."

"We'll see about that," I muttered. The drop from the edge of the roof still looked awfully far. My heart thumped faster as I tested my wings. They caught against the air with each flap, almost lifting me off the shingles already.

Good, sturdy wings. They'd carry me. I just had to take that leap of faith...

I pushed myself forward, over the eavestrough, out into the open air. My body plummeted with a lurch of my gut. A yelp broke from my throat. My arms flailed out, and my wings flailed too—flailed and swept against the air, cutting off my fall. I swooped upward, the wind rushing past me.

A giggle tumbled from my throat. I was flying. Really, truly flying.

As I lost momentum, I flapped my wings again, a little frantically and then with more confidence. Glide upward. Bank left. Some instinct deep inside me knew the right ways to move. I propelled myself back to where Loki was waiting.

"Well, look at you," he said. "What do you think?"

"I think," I said a little breathlessly, "I can go a hell of a lot higher than this."

I stretched my wings farther, pushing myself up toward the sky. A stronger wind buffeted me, and I soared on it, its warm fingers teasing across my wings. The waning sunlight streaked over my skin, the fresh country air filled my lungs, and for an instant, I felt invincible. I could go anywhere. Do anything.

I dove and swooped upward again, and the exhilaration made me giddy. I laughed, reveling in the sensation. Loki strode after me, walking on the air. When our gazes met, he was beaming at me, as if he was as pleased as I was with this new discovery.

"That's my girl," he said.

His voice was pleased, maybe even proud, but the words brought my mind back to earth. I *wasn't* his. I wouldn't let myself be. The only person I belonged to was me, no matter who had brought me back into this altered—and really kind of amazing—body.

I flapped my wings faster to send myself speeding up even higher into the sky. Up and up, until the air pressure started to lift and a strange sensation filled my ears.

Loki ascended with me. When I stopped, hovering with steady sweeps of my wings, he brandished his arm toward the landscape around us.

"I've passed on more than the power of transformation to you," he said. "You'll find your valkyrie senses are much more honed than you're used to. When you need to soar over battles, it helps to be able to zoom in on the details as you make your choices. Your eyes are sharper than a hawk's, your ears keener than a wolf's."

"Like yours?" I said.

He chuckled. "Oh, no one can beat mine. Take a look. See what you can see."

I hadn't had the opportunity to stretch my sight before. As I peered down over the world, distant shapes and colors came into sharper relief when I focused on them. There was the Hudson River snaking along to my left. That sprawling patch of gray off in the distance—in the space of a breath, my vision narrowed in on shining skyscrapers with glinting windows. New York City. Could I even hear the distant honking of its cars? No, that had to be someplace closer. There. My eyes narrowed in again on a farmstead to the west where someone was honking at a cow that had wandered onto the road, miles from here.

If New York was over there, that meant that Philadelphia would be... this way. I spun around as if simply enjoying the movement, but at the same time I noted the direction relative to the house for later use. My home city was too far for even these honed eyes to make out, but I could almost feel its hum. All those human lives my valkyrie senses were created to be attuned to.

"The whole world, opened up to you," Loki said. "Spectacular, isn't it?"

"Yes," I had to admit. My gaze roved across the fields, my ears perked. More cars wove along other roads around us. A plow rumbled across a field. Things I could see without any special focus. I frowned. "Don't we have to worry about regular people seeing *us*?"

Loki gave me a crooked smile. "You're part of the godly realm now, pixie. No mortal can see you unless you make a conscious effort to let them."

That was useful to know. I could fly anywhere then.

Bringing my attention back to my new body, I swooped and soared in another wide circle, swaying with the wind. Oh, this was spectacular, absolutely. I still wasn't sold on the whole wings thing while I was on the ground, but up here... Yeah, I'd keep them.

The shadows of the trees were stretching all the way

to the house now. A low rolling voice carried up to us from an open window.

"Loki! Get your ass down here for dinner. And ask Ari to please come too."

Loki motioned to me, still smiling. "Best not to get between Thor and his preferred dinner time. He's not the most pleasant company if you leave him hungry. Besides, I think you've come an awfully long way in one day."

"I have," I agreed as I soared with him toward the house. And I was going to go a whole lot farther the first moment I had the chance.

Tonight, if the gods slept, I could slip out of here without anyone noticing I'd left.

10

Aria

The pillow on my bed was so downy I almost wanted to burrow my head in it and give in to sleep. But my thoughts were still rattling through my head, keeping me way too alert, my body tensing and then relaxing at each creak of the house. I'd said I was exhausted from all the training I'd done today and headed up to the bedroom after dinner. Night had fallen outside the window now, stars showing against the deep black of the sky that I never really got in the city with the constant haze of streetlamps. I'd stopped hearing any sounds of movement an hour ago.

It seemed the gods did sleep. Which meant it was time for me to get moving.

I eased off of the bed and padded across the floor to the bedroom door. The hinges squeaked softly as I opened it. I winced and froze, but no one stirred in the rooms around and beneath me.

Had they really trusted me to just stay put? Maybe I'd put on a good enough show of enthusiasm today that they'd believed I'd bought into their whole plan completely. Not that I was going to assume as much and get careless. I had my own plans, my excuses all lined up.

I slipped down the hall to the dormer window that led onto the roof. The pane hissed open. I squeezed out into the warm night air.

Crickets were chirping somewhere below. Tiny glints of fireflies darted across the lawn, which was faintly lit by the light near-full moon. It was kind of pretty, if I'd come out here to admire the view. I crept away from the window across the pliant shingles and bowed my head.

The prickling, burning sensation of my emerging wings still made my nerves twitch, but I was getting used to it. Especially when I spread them and felt the air wafting against their feathers, the memory of how it had felt to soar up toward the sky that afternoon washing over me. My pulse gave a giddy leap.

I was going to feel that sensation again in a moment. And with luck I'd be seeing Petey not too long after that.

I sprang off the rooftop into the air with a flap of my wings. They caught the air before I even started to fall. I swept up over the house, inhaling sharply, the breeze streaking over my skin and ruffling my clothes.

For the first few minutes, I just glided around the house and yard, waiting to see what would happen. If the gods had some kind of safeguard in place, I could still play innocent, say I'd had trouble sleeping and wanted to practice my flying a little more. If I hadn't actually left the property, they couldn't accuse me of trying to flee.

But no one emerged from the house to see what I was doing. There was no sign that anyone had even noticed. I wet my lips. Could it really be this easy?

They might have ways of finding me after I woke up. I didn't know what all magic they were capable of. But maybe it wouldn't even come to that. I wasn't completely sure yet what I was going to do after I saw Petey. I could always sneak back here and go to bed as if I'd never left, and they wouldn't even know I'd gone. No point in trying to make a real run for it until I was sure I knew all the tricks I needed to evade them.

I took one last turn around the house, and then I banked to the right, pointing myself to the southwest. With a couple flaps of my wings, I was soaring toward home.

The wind raced over me, warbling in my ears. The landscape spilled out below me like I'd only seen before in aerial photographs. I grinned, reveling in the freedom.

And then a blob of shadow appeared in front of me, smacking into my body.

Cold tendrils wrapped around my limbs and my wings, weighing down on them. I yelped and struggled, but they resisted my efforts. The shadowy menace dragged me back down to earth.

Down to a field beyond the house where a dark-haired, dark-eyed god had his face tipped up to watch me fall.

The shadow didn't hurt me. It deposited me on the ground feet first with just a faint thump. But the cool clinging of its tendrils was making me shudder. I squirmed against it, trying to break free.

"Get this thing off me!"

"I don't think that you're in a position to make demands, valkyrie," Hod said in his flat voice. "I'll let you go when you tell me where *you* were going."

Would he even then? Somehow I doubted it. I forced my body to stop moving in the tangle of shadow and stared back at him through the thin moonlight. He was turned toward me, but like before, his gaze didn't quite meet mine. As if he thought I wasn't even worthy of that much acknowledgment.

"Don't lie," he added. "I know you were going *somewhere*. I waited to make sure you were leaving before I stopped you."

"Not much for sleeping, huh?" I said.

His gaze shifted, but it only seemed to move from my cheek to my forehead. "I'm the god of darkness," he said. "This is when I'm most awake."

"So you get to be the watchdog. Lucky you."

He ignored my jab. "Where were you going, valkyrie? If you'd like, we could take this discussion back to the house with the others. I'm sure Thor would be in an *excellent* mood woken up in the middle of sleeping off that dinner."

I let out a breath. I couldn't think of any lie that he'd believe that would go over better than the truth. "I was going home. Just to see how things are. I was going to come back."

"Sure you were," Hod said. "What exactly were you planning to do out there? Showing off how your new powers could help the criminals you've been hanging out with? Maybe stealing a thing or two?"

I bristled. Obviously Freya had reported our conversation to the others. And not in the most flattering terms.

"No," I snapped. "I'll be happy never to see the assholes I worked for again, and what the hell would I want to steal? I just want to make sure my little brother is okay. That's all. Sorry for having someone I can't just up and leave without even saying good-bye."

Hod blinked slowly. "Your little brother," he repeated.

"Yeah." My anger died down as I thought about Petey. "He's only six. And I'm basically the only person he can count on. He *needs* me. If he's heard I'm dead..." My throat choked up. I swallowed hard and managed to finish, a little raggedly. "I just need a few minutes with him. With all the stuff you guys want me to do for *you*, is that really too much to ask?"

The god was silent for a moment. I couldn't read the expression on his chiseled face, but at least he didn't look definitely pissed off anymore. His gaze slid farther to the side.

"No, it isn't," he said. "If that's really all this is about, you can go. But I'm coming with you."

He motioned, and the shadow that had clutched me released, slipping away from my skin. I rubbed my arms as if I could wipe the feeling of those cool tendrils from my memory. My body had tensed at the idea of having company for my visit. I didn't have much choice, though, clearly.

"Can you even fly?" I asked. "How do you figure you're going to keep up?"

His mouth slanted with a thin smile. "I'll manage. Lead the way."

I hopped off the ground with a tentative sweep of my wings, thinking I was going to have to go low and slow the whole way to the city. Beneath me, Hod made a tugging gesture toward him. The darkness of the night congealed around his feet into a thicker patch of shadow like the one he'd caught me with. He knelt on it, and it eased up into the air like some kind of bizarro flying carpet.

"Okay," I said, "I'll give you props for that. It's a pretty cool power. Is that what you're going to teach me in my valkyrie lessons?"

He grimaced. "No. Are we going, or did you change your mind?"

"Just trying to make conversation. Come on."

If he was going to be like that, I didn't really want to talk to him anyway. I soared up into the air with a few beats of my wings and pushed on toward Philly, not bothering to check whether Hod could keep up. He was a god. I shouldn't have to be holding back for him.

I sped across the landscape as fast as my wings would carry me, dipping down occasionally to check the highway signs and make sure I was on the right track. At maximum velocity, I could soar faster than the cars and trucks roaring along below me. When I bothered to glance back, Hod was keeping pace, perched securely on that patch of shadow, the wind only lightly ruffling his short black hair. He didn't look at me but somewhere farther in the distance.

Definitely not the friendly type. I guessed the other three had gotten all the charisma.

A familiar skyline came into view up ahead, and relief swelled in my chest. Part of me hadn't been convinced I'd even make it here until this moment. I flapped my wings even harder, putting in one last burst of speed to carry me the rest of the way home.

The scruffy-looking street outside Mom's scruffy-looking house was quiet as I dropped down onto the neighbor's roof. An old clunker sputtered past, and then the only noise was the faint rustle of the breeze through old Mrs. Jackman's laundry on the line out back. It had to be after midnight now.

Hod came to a stop beside me. He drifted over as I edged along the roof to where I could see Petey's window. His room was dark, but he'd left the curtains open, the window a few inches ajar. Like always.

Past evenings when I'd paid a stealthy visit, I'd scrambled onto the fence next door and then clambered the rest of the way using the ridge in the siding. Today I could be a little more graceful. I leapt with a stretch of my wings and glided onto that ridge, catching the window ledge with my hands.

Petey was asleep. I'd known he probably would be, but a twinge of disappointment ran through me anyway. His pale little face was slack, mushed against his pillow, his golden curls spilling every which way. His hand was clenched in a fist around the edge of his sheet.

It'd be mean to wake him up. He didn't look sad, at

least. No sign that he'd been crying. I'd only had fake ID on me when I'd been dropping off that package—the coroner or whoever might not even have figured out my real name.

I'd rather Petey never had to know exactly what had happened to me. As long as I could keep dropping in like I always had, he didn't have to know.

I wasn't going to wake him up, but I could leave him a sign that I'd been here. That I was thinking about him, always.

Hod had dipped down beside me on his flying shadow. "Where are you going now?" he said sharply when I left the window.

I shot him a glower. "To the corner store. To buy him a chocolate bar so he knows I came." I paused. "Well, to steal a chocolate bar, unless you happen to have some cash on you. When you summoned me, you guys didn't bother to summon the money I had on me when I died."

Hod made a face, but he fished in his pocket, produced a wallet, and offered me a five-dollar bill.

"Thanks!" I said brightly. "Are you babysitting me all the way to the store, too?"

"You haven't convinced me yet that you don't need the babysitting," he muttered. "You did try to take off on us *twice* this morning. How short do you think our memories are?"

I kept my voice sweet. "Well, you all did kind of materialize me out of some deathly void without any warning or explanation. Next time that happens, I'll be a little more chill about it, I promise."

Loki had told me I was invisible to mortals, but I

didn't totally believe it until I walked into the 24-hour shop a few blocks over and the lady working nights didn't even look up from the magazine she was reading behind the counter. I waved my wings in the air. Not a blink. Ha! Now if only the gods couldn't see me unless I wanted them to—then everything would have been a whole lot easier.

I grabbed a 3 Musketeers bar out of the row of boxes under the counter and tucked the five-dollar bill in its place. Payment and a tip.

Hod skulked after me the whole way back to Mom's house. I flapped back up to Petey's window and pushed it farther open with a creak of the frame. The screen had gotten torn years ago and Mom had never bothered to replace it, which had always suited me just fine. If she'd known how often I'd come in and out through this window over the last few years, she probably would have padlocked it shut.

Petey was so out he didn't even stir. I tiptoed over and tucked the chocolate bar under the end of his pillow. It'd been his favorite kind for the last two years, and I always joked with him that he and I were the two musketeers. "Two is all we need!" He'd know who had left it, no question.

Back at the window, I sat down on the ledge. I didn't really want to leave. Not right away. My brother's body hunched, small and fragile, under the blanket. The rasps of his sleeping breath washed over me.

"Are we done here?" Hod said where he was hovering outside.

"Give me a second," I said. "You're lucky I'm not asking to stay the whole night. Just look at him."

"I *can't*, even if I wanted to."

It took a second for me to process those words. My head jerked around. Hod gazed steadily back at me—except not into my eyes. Somewhere in the vicinity of my nose. Close, but not quite.

As if he couldn't quite pinpoint where my eyes even were.

I could have smacked myself. "You're blind."

"And you're not as observant as you'd like to think," Hod replied, but there wasn't much of an edge to the words. And it was a fair point.

"In my defense, I've been a little distracted in the last twenty-four hours," I said, and paused. "How did you follow me on the way out here? How did you even know I was leaving the house?"

He might have heard the window or me on the roof if his ears were good, but he'd said he'd waited until I left the property. I'd already been up in the air then.

Hod's lips twisted into something that wasn't quite a smile. "We brought you back to 'life'," he said. "We made you a valkyrie. That left a connection. If I concentrate, I can tell where you are. Any of the four of us could."

Oh. That made my whole escape plan a lot trickier. I wanted to ask whether distance affected this connection thingy, but that would only raise his suspicions. I could find a subtler way to figure that out later.

The god of darkness, always in the dark. Or *did* it look dark, if you simply couldn't see at all? Somehow I didn't get the feeling he wanted me prying into the intricacies of his blindness either.

I turned back to the bedroom. A murmur escaped Petey's mouth. He tucked his arm a little closer to his face. An ache spread through my chest, up to my throat.

I did have to go. But I'd be back. I swore it to any gods that actually existed, if there were more than the five I'd met so far.

My wings fluttered to hold me in place as I eased the window back to its previous position. Just in case Mom happened to be paying extra attention this morning. I pressed my fingers to my lips and then to the window as if Petey would feel that kiss on his forehead where I'd have wanted to press it.

A car engine growled down the street. A patchy red Chevy parked in front of the house, and a bulky figure swayed out of the passenger seat with a wave to whoever was driving. My shoulders stiffened.

Hod had turned toward the sound. "Who's that?" he asked.

"My mother's current boyfriend," I said. "Stoned to the eyeballs, it looks like."

Even as I was saying that, I realized I was wrong. His movements were clumsy, but in a jerky way. Twitchy. He looked *high*, not stoned. And high on something that wasn't treating him well.

It'd been a couple months since I'd last seen Ivan in person. How much had his habits changed since then?

He rattled the doorknob for a moment before he managed to get the key to work. Then he stomped inside. I held there for a minute, my wings flapping steadily in time with the too-loud thump of my heart. There wasn't anything I could do about that asshole.

I pushed my wings a little higher—and Ivan's voice bellowed through the house, raw and furious. "*Pete!*"

I flinched. Petey's bedroom door slammed open. My little brother woke with a jerk, pushing upright on the bed, his head listing as he dragged himself out of sleep.

"Where the hell did you put my controller, you little shit," Ivan roared. He barged through the room, flinging the blanket back on Petey's bed, swiping the toys off his play table in the corner. A Lego structure smashed on the floor.

"What?" Petey said, his voice wobbling. "I didn't take anything."

"You're always fiddling around with it," Ivan said. "It must have been you. Cough it up."

Petey cringed back on his bed, hugging his knees. "I really don't know. I didn't touch it today. I promise."

"Don't you fucking lie to me, you pathetic waste of space."

Ivan loomed over Petey, one bulging arm raised. A cry caught in my throat. I threw myself back at the window.

My fingers had just closed around the pane to yank it up when Ivan stepped back. His hand dropped to his side, his chest heaving with ragged breaths.

"Don't you dare mess with my stuff again," he growled, and thundered back out of the room.

A tear was streaking down Petey's cheek. He stifled a sob and heaved his blanket tight around him.

"Petey," I said, but he couldn't hear me either. Fuck,

how did this visibility thing even work? I was supposed to be able to let him see me if I wanted to—

I braced my arms to shove at the window pane, and a hand closed around my forearm.

"No," Hod said.

I glared back at him, even though I knew those fathomless dark green eyes couldn't see my expression. "You heard what just happened even if you couldn't see it. He's terrified."

"I can hear that it's over," Hod said. "And I don't think appearing before your brother as a winged magical being is going to put his mind at ease."

"Would you let me do it even if it would?" I asked.

He didn't answer that. "You have to let him go. You're not part of his world anymore. There's nothing you can really do for him." He hesitated. His voice thawed, just a little. "You showed him you care. That has to be enough."

As if on cue, Petey shifted his pillow and uncovered the chocolate bar. He snatched it up, a brilliant smile crossing his face. His gaze darted to the window, as if he were looking right at me. But he couldn't see *me*.

And yet he was beaming at me.

My heart squeezed, and Hod's grip tightened. I couldn't fight him. I already knew that.

At least, not like this.

I let him pull me back from the window. With a wrenching in my chest, I swept up into the sky.

The gods needed me right now. They wanted me to fulfill their mission. Fine. I'd track down Odin for them, and then they wouldn't need their valkyrie anymore. Maybe they'd be distracted enough that I could get away completely. Maybe they wouldn't even care at that point.

Either way, I was coming back here as soon as I could. And next time I'd do more than leave a chocolate bar.

11

Hod

I might not ever have seen a dawn, but I knew when it came. I could feel the moment the first rays of the sun seeped over the horizon like a faint but rising energy jittering over my skin, breaking through the stillness that had been the night.

No matter how many times I experienced that sensation, it always set my nerves a little on edge for the first few minutes. A vibration carried through the walls from the ceiling, a stirring in the bedroom above the study —Baldur's. My twin brother had been sleeping restlessly again, tossing and turning.

Nightmares, maybe. I didn't like to think about what those nightmares might contain. Whether I might feature in them, and how.

The chaos of the human world always agitated his

mind, even if he didn't complain about it. We'd been here too long. He needed the calm of Asgard.

A knock sounded on the study's half open door.

"Hod?" our new valkyrie said.

I turned in my chair to face her automatically, directing my eyes as well as I could to where I could sense her face was. It wasn't too hard to estimate from the direction and volume of her voice, from the soft sounds any body makes as it moves: the rustle of clothing, the rising and falling of breath. I'd formed a mental construct of her already from our earlier interactions—short and wiry and deft but forceful in action.

She'd contracted her wings. The soft murmur of those feathers would have been impossible to miss.

"Shouldn't you be in bed?" I said. We'd only returned a few hours ago from the reckless jaunt across the country I'd let her talk me into. I could get by on a nap or two throughout the day, but mortals—or those recently mortal —generally seemed to require more.

She shrugged, another rustle. It was a different shirt from yesterday, not the silvery hiss of silk but a somewhat coarser rasp I'd guess was cotton. "I got a little sleep. My mind decided I'm done." She paused. "You still need to teach me whatever it is you brought to making me a valkyrie."

"So you came for your lesson?"

"It seems like it's about time. Everyone else managed to fit theirs in yesterday."

She was shifting from her wary tone to the brasher one I was becoming equally used to. I'd have thought our valkyrie had only two modes if I hadn't heard her voice soft with affection at her little brother's window last night.

I was already regretting the decision to let her go see him. She hadn't been up to anything nefarious, that much was true—this time. But her ties to her old life clearly remained tight, and venturing back into it had only strengthened them. I didn't believe she was eager to learn so she could fulfill our mission. Loki had chosen her because she was like him—a sly one, a schemer. No doubt from the moment I'd sent her back toward this house last night she'd been forming new plans of her own.

That damned choked sound she'd made when she'd mentioned her brother had swayed my resolve for one imprudent moment.

She took a step closer, swiveling to take in the room. "What are you doing in here anyway? You can't read all these books, right?"

I propped one elbow against the desk and the other on the back of my chair. "I can in a way." With the right supernatural compulsion, I could make the ink murmur its words to me. "We all find ways of adapting."

She hummed to herself. "I'm going to guess that's not what you're going to teach me, though."

"No." I *was* going to have to teach her, regardless of her motives for asking, but that didn't mean now was an ideal time for it. "I think it would be better if you were fully rested first. What I have to show you is... more discomforting than what you'll have learned from the others." Which was why I hadn't rushed in to provide my part earlier.

"Well, now you've really peaked my curiosity. I'm

definitely not getting back to sleep with that idea in my head. Might as well get it over with!"

She wasn't going to give up. Why was I wasting my time arguing? If she wanted to learn so badly, let her find out for herself.

I pushed myself to my feet. "If you insist."

Just the thinnest warmth was starting to creep through the window. A row of small potted ferns sat along the sill. I let my fingers come to rest on the delicate fronds of the nearest one and motioned for the valkyrie to join me.

"You've talked with the others about the traditional duties of the valkyries," I said.

She nodded, a whisper of her hair, as she came up beside me. She was close enough now that I could smell her as well as hear her: clean and hot and ever so slightly sharp, the way fire smelled beneath the smoke. Had that come with her transformation into a valkyrie, or had it always been her natural scent?

"The basics," she said. "Watch the battles, choose the winners, send the deserving up to Valhalla. That about covers it, right?"

"It does. But only on the surface level. You don't just choose the winners—you choose the losers as well. And what happens to the losers in a war? What happens to those deserving before they ascend?"

"They die," she said. "Obviously."

"And when a valkyrie chooses, sometimes she's the one who takes that life." I stroked my hand over the fern. It tickled my fingertips. "Your new senses will allow you to feel the hum of life inside a body. You gather it in your grasp and then you ease it all the way out. There's a darkness in you that can swallow it whole."

The living energy in the fern quivered at my touch. I curled my fingers as if I were physically gathering it against my palm. The fronds trembled and turned dry against my hand. The warmth of that energy cooled as it congealed. I closed my hand into a fist—and it was gone. The fern was nothing more than a limp husk. Nausea unfurled in my gut.

Loki's plan still seemed like another of his harebrained risks as likely to blow up in our faces as get us where we needed to go. But, by the Allfather, wherever he was, I hoped this valkyrie would be the last one we needed. If only so I never had to carry out this tutorial again.

"I could do that?" Ari said. She sounded unnerved. Good.

"You wouldn't be a valkyrie if you couldn't. This is the lesson. Now it's your turn."

She shifted, reaching toward one of the other ferns. After a moment of silence, she said, "I don't think I feel what you were talking about."

"I can help," I said briskly. This was what I was here for. I'd just have to get it over with.

I set my hand over her smaller one, the smooth skin of her knuckles brushing my palm. The darkness in me reached out to the sliver of the void running through her being. Teased it closer to the surface of her awareness. Set the plant's energy thrumming in contrast.

Ari sucked in a breath. "Oh."

I eased back, letting her instincts guide the process

from there. Somewhere inside her, she already knew what to do.

A shiver ran through her body. Her hand clenched. I let mine slide to the fern beneath. It had crumpled like the one I'd killed.

"And that works on anything living?" she said. "Just like that?"

"Any life can be snuffed out. Or cast from its body toward Valhalla, although those doors aren't open to mortal souls any longer."

"Got it." She let out a jagged chuckle. "Now that's an ability I wish I'd had on call last night!"

I tensed. My fingers leapt to close around her wrist, yanking her so she faced me. "*Never* treat the taking of a life lightly. In a battle where someone has to die, you make that choice. That's the only time you do. You can't go stealing away lives out of nowhere."

"Okay, okay," she said. "It was a joke. A bad one, obviously." The strands of her hair murmured as she cocked her head. "And a sore spot for you."

"Not one that's any of your business."

"That doesn't mean I can't be curious."

"It means I've got nothing to say about it," I said. My lungs had already started to constrict. "Drop it, valkyrie. And don't joke like that again."

"Fine. I'm sorry."

She was silent then, for a moment that stretched into another and then another. I realized I was still holding onto her wrist and released it. Ari inhaled slowly, but still she didn't speak. Her silence niggled at me.

"What's the matter, valkyrie?" I asked. Let her spit

out whatever her complaint was. She thought I was being too harsh? She didn't like having her questions cut off? Let her try me. I could remind her what her place was here. That she hadn't been owed a place here at all.

The shape of her voice suggested a grimace. "What makes you think there's something wrong?"

"You got quiet," I retorted. "Normally you're as bad as Loki, the way you go on."

She exhaled. "I was just wondering why you don't really look at me. Not *look at me* look at me—I know you can't see. But I've watched you with the other gods. You can at least make it seem as if you're meeting their eyes. But you don't with me. Like I'm so much beneath you, you can't be bothered."

The anger I'd been stoking faltered. That wasn't at all what I'd expected. She hadn't said how that impression affected her, but her discomfort was threaded through her voice.

"It's not you," I said. "Well, it is, but it's only that I'm not as familiar with you. I've had hundreds of years to build a model of each of them in my head, to fine tune it. I have less experience to draw on with you. I have to approximate more."

Her posture unclenched. I hadn't realized how much I'd unsettled her. "Well," she said, "it seems like there's an easy way we could fix that."

Her hand closed around mine and drew it to her face. She rested my palm lightly against her cheek. My fingertips brushed the scattered waves of her hair. Her eyelashes grazed the pad of my thumb when she blinked. And just like that, the construction of her in my head reconfigured itself in infinitely more detail. Detail that included the soft warmth of her skin against mine. The way her breath tingled over the inside of my wrist. All the life in *her* sang beneath that surface.

A pang shot through me in response.

"Wonderful," I said in a voice I could already tell was too curt, aiming my blank gaze at where I now knew her eyes to be. "Familiarity increased. Lesson concluded. Just hope you never need to use that one."

"That's it?" she said.

I nodded to the door, that motion just as curt. "You can go."

It was an order, not an offer. She made a brief disgruntled sound, but she went. I waited until I was sure she'd left the hall, and then I went out after her. An uneasy energy stirred through my body and gnawed at the dull ache that pang had left behind.

I knew the house well enough after all this time that I could move through it without hesitation. My model of it was near-perfect. The creak of the floor and the vibrations that ran through the boards told me when a piece of furniture might have changed position, though they rarely did. Nothing hindered me on my way to Loki's bedroom door.

The sounds of motion on the other side told me he was up. I strode inside, greeted by his huff.

"Just because you can't *see* doesn't mean a person can't still want a little privacy," he said, his voice momentarily muffled by the shirt he was pulling on.

I snorted. "You're the last one to ever think of anyone else's privacy, aren't you? I just wanted to tell you that your valkyrie has all her training. So let's get on with things."

Loki chuckled. "What a hurry you're in all of a sudden."

"We all want to get back to Asgard," I said. That was the only thing I wanted right now. Baldur was becoming more detached with each week longer we were trapped here. Back in those even more familiar halls, we could all stop this constant fretting. And we could get away from mortals and valkyries and the lot of them.

Away from the strange sense of longing this valkyrie in particular had somehow managed to provoke in me.

"Hmm," Loki said, in that way he had as if he knew far more than he ought to. "While she's coming along well, I don't think it'd be fair to throw her into the fray quite yet. But I might have just the thing for a final test."

12

_____

Aria

It was already late in the day when we reached our destination: a small, faded-looking industrial city somewhere in the north end of Michigan. Shadows clung to the vacant factories with boarded up windows we passed. We walked through the streets, invisible to mortal eyes, but the truth was in this part of town there wasn't much of anyone around to see us.

I peered through the gap where one warehouse's front door sagged on its hinges. The dwindling sunlight didn't penetrate the interior at all. A smell like grease and chalk mixed together hung in the air, and traffic rumbled along the highway a few blocks over. When I extended my senses, the mass of human lives—all that living energy I could steal into the shadow inside me if I got close enough—hummed around me at a distance.

A cheerful scene, this was not.

"What are we looking for?" I asked. All Loki had said about this trip so far was that we needed to wait until it started to get dark before we could take much action. I'd dozed as much as I could to prepare for this apparent test, and then trained a little more: sparring with Thor, testing the limits of my wings on my own. Not knowing what the test *was*, it was hard to know how to prepare.

"It's come to my attention that a warg has been roaming around this bit of Midgard," Loki said. He brushed a rotting cardboard box aside with his foot, his lips curling in distaste. "You'll track it down, corner it, and overpower it. If you can manage that, I think you're ready for whatever might wait you when you go looking for Odin."

"Great," I said. "Wonderful. What the hell is a warg?"

"And why didn't you mention to the rest of us that one was causing trouble?" Hod demanded from where he was stalking along at the edge of our group.

"A warg is a monster that looks a lot like one of your wolves," Thor said to me. He'd kept close beside me since we'd entered the city, his bulky body like a shield. "But bigger, faster, fiercer, and smarter."

"Oh. Well, that sounds like fun." I bet I didn't get to keep him as my shield when I went after this one.

"And I didn't mention it because it only recently started causing enough trouble for us to bother interfering," Loki said. "Mortal eyes see only a stray dog. It's broken into a few stores and apartments scrounging for food. Nothing too horrifying. But it seems to be developing an interest in fresh meat. It savaged a little girl last night. And I'd hate to think what may have been happening to the pet population in the area."

My back had gone rigid. A little girl. I guessed one life didn't mean much to the gods who'd watched billions come and go, but that was all I needed to hear to consider this more than just a test.

"All right. Let me at it."

"Patience, pixie," Loki said. "I don't want us spending all night on a tracking mission. I'll get you close enough that you should be able to follow the trail fairly quickly."

"One can't help wondering when it was you found the time to be keeping an eye on this creature," Freya said from where she was strolling along behind us. Even though she hadn't been part of my training directly, she'd scoffed at the idea that we leave her behind. *It's my husband she'll be looking for. I'd like to have some say in whether she's ready.*

"Oh, I'm capable of keeping track of all sorts of things with very little effort," Loki said loftily.

"And you have an affinity for wolves, after all," Baldur remarked in his airy way.

The trickster god cut his gaze toward Baldur, his shoulders tensing, but the god of light barely seemed to notice his apprehension, so I doubted he'd meant to cause it. "Yes," Loki said. "There is that."

Was that one of the shapes Loki could shift into? It would suit him. I was going to ask, but then he stopped by a wide alley that stretched between two brick factory buildings and raised his chin toward it. "That way," he said. "You take the lead now. Let's see how much you've learned, pixie."

Oh, I'd show them, all right. Honestly, I was a little curious to find out myself. This was my first chance to try out these skills on an actual menace.

I wanted to get on with the whole finding Odin thing, but I wasn't going to be any good to Petey if I died all over again in the process. So I couldn't exactly argue with the gods' wariness to throw me straight into whatever had swallowed up the other valkyries they'd sent looking.

I edged down the alley, tucking my hand into my pocket and drawing out my switchblade. I didn't know how much good that four-inch blade would do against a warg, but it was more likely to do damage than my bare hands were. And the warmed plastic against my palm steadied me.

Maybe I hadn't been able to use this weapon to protect myself as much as I should have, back when it had really mattered, but I could make it count now.

As I scanned the alley, my heightened senses directed my attention. My gaze caught on a tuft of coarse fur clinging to the corner of a brick. At shoulder height, where some massive furred body must have brushed against these walls. A murky, musky smell crept into my nose.

I swallowed hard and kept going. My five spectators trailed along behind me, giving me a ten-foot lead and total silence.

The alley split like the head of a T, left and right. I glanced in each direction, watching, listening, tasting the air. Only a hint of a breeze stirred the muggy atmosphere, but I caught a hint of that murky scent from the right—where my perked ears also picked up a panted breath from somewhere far down that dirty concrete path through this industrial maze.

I skirted a dumpster that looked like it hadn't been used in years but still gave off a stale stink and picked my way between the buildings. Disintegrating shreds of wood and warped bits of metal scattered the cracked cement. The factories and warehouses loomed on either side, cutting off the sun completely. Only a narrow line of gray-blue sky showed above me.

Another rough breath led me around a second turn. The smell got thicker in my oversensitive nose.

Up ahead, a few hulking metal machines had been put out to pasture in a concrete yard surrounded by a chain-link fence. Something had torn a gash in that fence near the alley—a gash as tall as I was and twice as wide.

The shadow beneath one of the machines shifted. It wasn't all shadow. A huge dark shape was slumped there. Taking its rest before its nighttime prowl?

My mouth went dry. My fingers tightened around the handle of my switchblade. I eased through the gash in the fence, not even daring to look back and confirm the gods were still following me. My gaze never left the beast cloaked in the shadow.

I couldn't tell what the machine casting the shadow might have been meant for. It was a jumbled structure of rusted metal panels, looping tubes, and cylinders that might have spun once but now were locked in place with grit and their own share of rust. The contraption farther beyond it looked like a massive sewing machine, taller than me, with a steel "needle" as thick as my wrist.

The form in the shadow had to be at least twice as large as I was. My sharpened eyes could only just make out the tips of its thick pelt along the edge of its body. How the hell was I supposed to "overpower" that thing?

What did I have that it didn't? My wings. I extended them with a swift unfurling, ignoring the biting burn that came with pushing them out so quickly. I could always fly out of reach if I needed to. Herd it from above. *Corner it*, Loki said. And then... trap it somehow?

Or kill it, using the power Hod showed me this morning?

It'd been attacking kids. A monster like that needed to be put down—if I could pull that skill off when it was a huge, fast creature and not just a plant sitting still in a pot.

I was only halfway to the shadow when the monster lifted its head: an immense, wolfish head with pointed ears and a glint of teeth along its muzzle. It growled low in its throat.

And then it charged.

I leapt out of the way with a heave of my legs and a flap of my wings, only my enhanced valkyrie strength pushing me far enough to dodge the swipe of the warg's claws. It spun on me and lunged again. I fluttered higher into the air with a lurch of my heart. Its jaws snapped shut just below my heel.

Fuck. If I'd had any doubts about whether this thing needed to be destroyed, they'd vanished now. The question wasn't so much whether I was going to kill it as how I was going to while making sure it didn't devour me.

The beast circled the yard beneath me as I swept higher still, pulling myself well out of range to gather my thoughts. I had strength and speed, flight and heightened senses. And the ability to sense emotions, intentions—Baldur's gift.

Dragging in a breath, I focused on the monster. On the pulse of vicious energy inside its head.

It had sensed what I was here to do. It planned to end me before I ended it. Even now, it was gathering itself for a jump at me.

I could read that: what move it would make next. If I could feel that out, I could stay one step ahead of it and dive for its weak spots the first chance I got.

Which meant I had to get closer again.

I flitted out of the way of its leap and then dropped back to the ground. The warg whirled, bounding left and then right, a feint and a jab. But I'd seen that coming. I rolled out of the way, stabbing out with my switchblade. The blade sank into the flesh just behind the creature's foreleg before I yanked my weapon back.

The warg snarled and whipped toward me. Blood dappled the pavement. My pulse beat fast and hard through my veins. I just had to keep this up, had to keep weakening it, until I got a bigger opening. I could do this. For myself. For Petey. For the little girl this monster had hurt.

It sprang at me with a gnash of its teeth, just at the moment I'd felt to expect it. I dodged and slashed out at its other side. The beast swung around so quickly my knuckles brushed its side before I could pull myself away. My eyes connected with the warg's for a single instant. For long enough to take in their flat yellow sheen—and a cold gleam of intelligence shining behind them.

As if there were a human being behind that monstrous face, staring back at me.

My stomach flipped. My wings flapped instinctively, propelling me up and away. At the same moment, another darkly furred body hurtled at me from the top of one of the abandoned machines.

A gasp jolted out of me, and then clawed feet were slamming me into the concrete. I thrashed and rolled, squirming away just as teeth grazed my cheek, digging my heels into a furry gut and heaving back against it with all the strength Thor had passed on to me. Pain lanced down my face with a wet chill, but the warg on me stumbled back just far enough for me to scramble out from under it. Right into the lunge of a third.

Three of them. There were three of them.

I spun around, swaying as I caught my balance, my palm gone clammy against the handle of my switchblade. My fist smacked my latest attacker's muzzle to the side, but only by a few inches. And the other two were closing around me again.

I couldn't do this. Couldn't take on all of them. I'd needed all my strength and concentration just to fight the first. I threw myself up toward the sky, spreading my wings—and a monstrous jaw clamped hard around one wing tip.

Teeth raked through feathers and flesh, dragging me back to earth. Pain splintered through those unfamiliar nerves and into my back. I cried out, panicked adrenaline shooting through my body, and slashed out with my hand with all the desperate force I could summon.

A crackle of lightning seared down my arm and along the blade, blasting into the monster's side and sending it flying across the yard. Its body smashed into one of the machines and crumpled to the ground, motionless.

What the *fuck* had that been? I didn't have time to ask, to experiment. Another warg was barreling into me. I stumbled to the side, hissing at the slice of its claws through my calf. My hand waved the switchblade wildly, but wherever I'd summoned that lightning from, I didn't know how to call it up again.

I was not going to die here. Not again. I *was not*. It just wasn't an option.

I swept my leg around, slamming it heel first into an incoming warg's snout. My valkyrie strength sang through my muscles, seeming to blaze hotter with the blood pulsing from my wounds and my enemies'.

The warg snapped at me again, and I dove right under its jaws with a speed I wouldn't have believed anyone could be capable of a couple days ago. My blade cut across the beast's throat.

Not deeply enough. More blood pattered down on me, but the creature staggered to the side, still growling. Where the hell was the other one?

Before I could whirl to check, the one I'd wounded was charging at me. A haze of pain emanated from its head. I'd weakened it. I had to take the advantage while I had it.

I leapt aside and heaved at the beast's shoulder with

all my might. It staggered and sprawled on its side. I sprang onto it, willing all the strength in my body to weigh it down as I jammed the tip of my blade against the softest part of the creature's throat.

The flickering life energy of the monster washed over me, heavier and brighter than both Hod's ferns and the people in the city around us but with the same heady tingling. It flailed its limbs, and I slammed my elbow into the joint of its foreleg with a force that made the bone snap. Then, with a ragged breath, I dug my fingers into the coarse fur and hauled at that energy with the darkness already unfurling in my chest.

The warg's eyes rolled back, but the light didn't entirely fade from them. The one I could see slid to meet my eyes. Suddenly I was sure, down to my bones, this was the same one I'd locked eyes with before. The first one I'd tangled with. That sense of cold but clear intelligence washed over me again—thoughts as sharp and certain as the ones in my own head. A consciousness on par with mine, that I was about to extinguish forever.

A shiver ran down my spine. My grip on the creature's ruff and its life wavered, just for an instant.

The monster sensed that split-second of hesitation and bucked with a gnash of its jaws.

My body jolted. I slid and almost tumbled from my hold. My hand whipped back just a hair from disappearing into that maw. My other hand clenched its fur with renewed determination. With one last, frantic yank, I wrenched the life from the warg's body.

The dark space inside me swallowed that energy

whole. The creature beneath me slumped. My body slumped too, a sob hitching from my throat.

The third warg had wheeled and fled. I saw a flash of its tail as it raced down an alley on the opposite side of the yard, and then I was alone there with the bodies of the two I'd killed.

Two monsters. But the ache spreading from beneath my ribs wasn't victorious at all.

13

Aria

The gods were still arguing around me when we reached the house in the middle of the night.

"The point is you told her there was one," Thor said with a sweeping gesture of his broad arm, his voice not much more than a growl. "You purposely left her underprepared. We were supposed to be testing her, not throwing her to the wolves—literally."

"And we did test her," Loki said evenly. "She proved she could handle herself even if the odds shifted even more against her. Even if her enemies multiplied or came on her unexpectedly. From what I saw, it was the wolves that got thrown."

"Just like always," Hod muttered. "You set up some precarious scheme and then act as if it wasn't just dumb luck it worked out in your favor."

Loki shook his head. "If our valkyrie should be

offended by anything, it's your apparent lack of faith in her."

"What's done is done," Baldur said. He gave me a warm if slightly distant smile. I thought it had gotten a little thinner as the arguing had continued. "Let's not dwell on it. Why don't we focus on the good that's come of this? Aria succeeded—very well. We should celebrate that victory."

I didn't feel much like celebrating. All but the worst of the wounds the wargs had left me with had closed up of their own accord, another surprise valkyrie ability, and Baldur's gentle touch had washed away the rest along with any lingering pain, but I was still wiped out. My body was ready to collapse into bed... and my head was still cluttered with too many jostling thoughts for me to think I'd actually fall asleep.

Freya slipped in beside me and tucked her hand around my elbow. "I think what our valkyrie needs is a little time away from the lot of you," she said, sweetly but firmly. "It's been a long, tense night, Ari. A walk will help you wind down."

I was too distracted by the jumble in my head to protest when she guided me away from the others, across the lawn toward the same path we'd strolled along earlier. When my mind caught up, apprehension prickled over my skin. Was she going to pump me for more information? Make sure my motives had been pure or who knew what else?

I was trying to figure out the smoothest way to extricate myself when she glided to a stop just beyond the first cluster of trees and turned to face me. Her deep blue eyes peered into mine, but her gaze was soft rather than sharp.

"That was hard for you," she said. "And not just physically."

Emotion swelled inside me: relief that someone at least partly understood, panic that she'd decide it made me unworthy somehow. What would they do with me if they didn't think I could complete this quest for them after all?

I grappled for words. "I've never killed something like that before. Something... The wargs aren't just animals, are they? Not regular ones. It felt almost like I was killing a person."

Freya's mouth twisted. My sense of her mental state was faint and vague, but the concerned vibe I did pick up felt nothing but genuine. Was she actually *worried* about me? And if she was, was it for my sake, or for how it would affect their plans?

"They're beasts," she said. "Vicious, driven by animal-like instincts to dominate and devour. But yes, they can think more than the beasts you're used to. That doesn't mean they should get to live doing whatever they please."

"No." But it also didn't mean I was going to feel ecstatic about having to be the one to cut those thoughts off permanently.

"You'll need to be prepared," she said. "If enemies of Asgard have captured Odin, they'll be monsters of a similar sort. Even closer to human, most likely. But they've already cut down three before you. They won't show *you* any mercy."

"Oh, I'm not going to be merciful when someone's coming for my throat. No guilt over that, believe me." Just a vaguely unsettled feeling I hadn't been able to shake yet.

A feeling that had dislodged a whole bunch of other uncomfortable thoughts. Freya started walking again, at a more leisurely pace, and a question that had been nagging at me for a while now tumbled out.

"Can you—can the gods die? You call us 'mortals,' but... I don't remember my mythology all that well, but I know there were prophecies about deaths and all that."

"We can," Freya said. "Most of us did, during Ragnarok, although I can't say it was much more pleasant for those who simply witnessed the entire thing. But those who died returned to life in the aftermath of the destruction."

"So even if you die, you come back," I said.

"Well, we aren't entirely sure what would happen if any of us were pushed to the brink again. We knew Ragnarok was coming. It was meant to be. What's to follow has never been clear." She rubbed her mouth. "Some of us might have vanished already. There are others of Asgard we haven't spoken to in centuries."

The next question I was almost afraid to ask, but I had to.

"Are you sure *Odin* hasn't been cut down like those other valkyries were? That wherever he is, whatever's happened to him, he's still alive?"

That you're not searching for someone who can no longer be found?

Freya's jaw tightened a little, but her voice stayed

mild. "I would know. If his essence had departed the realms... I would know. As would the others, I expect, maybe even more sharply than I would."

Okay. That explanation sounded like new-age blathering to me, but it wasn't as if I didn't know that the gods had senses beyond what I'd been used to. I could take her word for it.

"So you're stuck here just waiting for him." I tried to imagine it—the existence of a god. What my existence would theoretically look like, if I managed not to get myself killed on this mission of theirs. "Does it get... *boring*, being around this long? What do you even *do*? I mean, when you don't have a valkyrie around to put through the paces."

Freya laughed. Her amusement felt genuine too. "Oh, I'm sure we all have our moments of boredom. But humans provide endless new entertainment and drama, and this is just one of the nine realms. We all have our pet subjects. Baldur follows music; Thor enjoys sports. Norns know what mischief Loki is occupying himself with at any given time. Hod collects all the latest manuscripts on philosophy and scientific inquiry—a strange combination, I'd say, but he doesn't ask my opinion."

I kind of wanted to bristle at the idea of people like me being around just for the entertainment of a bunch of gods, but then, maybe it wasn't that different from watching reality TV? If we did it to ourselves, I couldn't really get mad at them over it.

"What about you?" I asked.

"Oh..." Her gaze turned distant. "It's always

interesting to see the directions fashion rambles off in and returns to. But mostly my expertise is love. Romantic and motherly. I intervene on occasion, when a misunderstanding seems a little too tragic or when I can help a child come to be." Her smile came back, a little bittersweet this time. "I just have to be careful not to get *too* invested. I'm not a meddler on Loki's scale."

It didn't really seem right that the goddess of love should have a husband who apparently wandered off doing who knew what for ages at a time. How lonely must she get? I had enough sense of self-preservation not to ask that out loud, but I couldn't help prodding a bit. "I guess it's hard without Odin here."

"Well, it's not as if I hadn't seen what he was like before we forged that connection." She glanced at me. "Before you think I'm all soft-bellied sap, I should mention my other specialty is war. It was skirmishes and battles that Odin and I first bonded over. Believe me, if I could be the one taking the risks we're asking you to, leaping into the fray to find him, I'd charge forth without a second's hesitation. I wish I could."

As she said it, I saw the steel in her under that dolled-up exterior. She meant *that*, unquestionably. She didn't like having to ask me to go in her place.

I'd already had every intention of surviving for my own benefit, but I felt compelled to say, to show her the steel I had too, "I'm not going to get caught like the valkyries before. I'll figure out what happened to him, and I'll make it back. You can count on that much."

"You know, after tonight's performance, I think perhaps I can." She stopped again and touched the side of my arm. "Thank you for doing what I can't. I'm sorry you didn't have more of a choice in the matter. You seem more settled now. Would you like to get back to the house? If you're hungry, we may be able to scrounge up a few bits of food Thor hasn't already devoured."

"I think I need to sleep more than I need to eat right now." I had to fight to suppress a yawn.

We headed back to the house in a weird sort of companionable silence. Weird because I couldn't remember the last time I'd just walked in silence with someone and not felt like I needed to be totally on guard.

Freya wasn't all that bad, really. I was pretty sure I wasn't ever going to need to stab her, in any case.

A flicker of movement beyond the house's roof caught my gaze. A dark flutter against the equally dark treetops. I narrowed my eyes, calling on my valkyrie senses. The details of branches and leaves sharpened to reveal a shape swooping from one perch to another. A hawk.

Another dropped down out of the night sky to join it. I frowned. Hawks were daytime birds, weren't they? What were two of them doing suddenly hanging out around the gods' house in the middle of the night? And the energy I sensed in them had a deliberateness to it that sent an uneasy prickling down my back. It set off a deeper tremor in my gut, something hotly insistent. An instinct I didn't know how to read.

"What?" Freya asked, taking in my expression.

"There are two hawks in that tree," I said, nodding to it. "Something about them doesn't feel right. Like they're watching the house." And like they should mean something to me. I just didn't know what.

EVA CHASE

Freya's expression hardened. In that moment, she looked every inch the war goddess. "You've been tested enough today," she said. "When you get inside, tell Loki I could use a hand. Then go enjoy that bed of yours. You've earned it."

"What are you going to do about them?" I asked.

The corner of her lips curled upward. "I can be very charming when I want to be. And once they're charmed down here, I'm sure our trickster can determine what tricks they're up to. If it's anything all that exciting, you'll hear about it in the morning."

14

Thor

I was on my third slice of breakfast ham when Loki sauntered into the kitchen. Somehow, even when he was doing something as innocent as pouring himself a cup of coffee, he always managed to look as if he were up to no good. I supposed I should just be glad that in recent memory he'd always been scheming on our side.

"Did you glean anything else from that hawk?" I asked.

"Nothing more than confirming what I'd already seen," Loki said. "It had a tang of rot on it, even though the bird itself was lively enough, and a shiver of unfriendly magic. Neither of which I like, but neither of which is all that catastrophic at this point."

"No creatures like that ever came around here before."

"No," Loki said. "I do have to wonder if that little battle last night caught someone's attention."

I looked up from my ham. "Like who?"

He gave me a narrowly amused look. "If I knew that, I'd already be knocking on their door, not discussing it with you."

"But you think they might be after Ari."

"Or interested in her, at least. She did surprise even us, after all."

Her blast of lightning. The last three valkyries hadn't displayed that talent. I'd had no idea I could pass on my affinity for the stuff that literally, but clearly I had. And with a similar lack of control. She'd used it on instinct, the same way the battle rage came over me.

Baldur drifted into the kitchen with a gentle nod to both of us on his way to the fridge to retrieve a hard-boiled egg. I nodded in return and refocused on Loki. "And you haven't had any thoughts on how *that* could have happened?"

Loki spread his hands. "No more than you. Perhaps you always passed on a spark, and none of the others ever had enough spirit for it to really take light. She does have rather a lot of fire."

"Yes," Baldur said in his light voice, joining me at the table. "She's been quite impressive."

"She has," I agreed. If I hadn't been so worried about Ari's fate last night, I might have enjoyed being awed by how quickly she'd gotten comfortable with her new strength and speed. I'd have taken her as a fighting partner any day. Holding her own against not one but *three* wargs...

A little of yesterday's anger tickled up with that memory.

"Your theory seems to have been right," Baldur added, smiling at Loki. "Perhaps character isn't half so important as determination and adaptability."

"I think Ari has plenty of character too," I said. "And I'll give Loki more credit when he proves he's not going to kill her before she gets a chance to do what we've been training her for."

Loki waved off my complaint as he took a gulp of his coffee. He always drank it fast and scalding hot. "Stop your fretting. She was fine. And if she hadn't been, the five of us were right there. I'd like to think at least one of us would have been quick enough to intervene if she'd looked as though she needed it."

Had he been thinking that the whole time we'd been watching? I probably would have jumped in if I'd seen one of the monsters about to land a fatal blow, but I'd have done it expecting Loki to chide me afterward for ruining the test.

I scowled at myself. I'd accepted what I'd thought were his rules too quickly, hadn't I? He might have a faster wit, but he wasn't any more in charge around here than the rest of us were.

If Hod had been here, he'd have some dark comment at the ready to match my mood. But the god of night usually slept not long after dawn. We wouldn't see him for at least a couple hours.

"I still say it was a dirty trick."

Loki grinned. "And I'd say there's no such thing as a clean one. Do you think our enemies are going to play fair? If they had, those pure-of-heart girls we summoned would have fared much better."

He was right. That didn't mean I had to like it. "Oh, shut up," I muttered.

"You all should shut up," Freya declared, sweeping into the room. The scent of honeysuckles trailed after her like it always did when she'd been exercising her powers. Charming that wretched hawk down—some task for a love goddess.

"And why exactly is that?" Loki asked, cocking his head.

"Still having the same stupid argument." Freya gestured toward the hall. "If you're so worried about the girl, why don't you pay a little more attention to what she's going through *now* instead of what she's already been through and come out the other side of. The lot of you didn't have the faintest idea how unsettled she was *after* she survived last night, did you?"

I blinked. "Of course she was a little shaken. But once Baldur looked after her wounds..."

"She seemed to prefer time to process on her own," Baldur said. "I gave her that space."

"Because that's all she's used to, not because that's what's good for her!" Freya sighed and shook her head. "It's amazing you men manage to get anything done, I swear. Three days ago she was a regular human being, and the next thing she knows she's fighting deadly monsters she wouldn't have thought belonged anywhere other than myths. I had a talk with her last night, but I think she's still struggling. She's already up, you know.

She's been sitting on the roof for the last hour just watching the sky."

Oh. I'd assumed I hadn't seen Ari because she was still sleeping. Even Loki looked mildly chagrined, though I wasn't convinced he'd completely missed everything Freya had mentioned. Maybe he simply hadn't thought it worth bothering with. Who knew with the Mischief Maker?

If anyone here knew how to deal with the aftermath of a battle, it was me. I pushed back my chair. "I'll go see what she needs."

Freya crossed her arms. "Just keep in mind she probably needs a *subtle* touch, Thunderer."

"I can be subtle," I retorted. But the truth was, subtlety wasn't exactly my strong point. I paused in the hall, considering my possible tactics. Then I hustled up the stairs to retrieve something from my room before I headed out the door.

It was another fine summer day—finer than the last few, really. The humidity had died down, leaving a heat that was more crisp than suffocating. Birds were chirping and fluttering between the trees. All except the one the hawks had been perched in last night, I couldn't help noticing. That didn't bode well.

I circled the house, tapping my thigh with a solid thunk of the object I was carrying. It grounded me, reminded me of my strengths. I might not be a smooth talker like Loki or filled with gentle light like Baldur, but I'd spent enough time around our valkyrie to have a decent idea where to start if she needed steadying.

Ari was where Freya had said she'd be, perched by

the edge of the roof outside the third-floor dormer. Her blond waves were swept back from her face, and she had her head tipped back to soak up the sun. It was hard to judge her expression at that distance.

"Hey, Ari!" I hollered. "You look like you could use something to do."

Her gaze darted down. A grin flashed across her face when she saw me. "What did you have in mind?" she shouted back.

I shrugged. "Come down, and I'll show you."

She stood up, and her wings unfurled from her back with a rush of rustling feathers, no hesitation now. As casual as could be, she stepped off the end of the roof. Her wings caught the air just enough to turn what should have been a fall into a swift glide. She landed in front of me with a thump of her feet and an arch of her eyebrows.

"Here I am. Show away."

I'd agreed that she'd been impressive last night, but that was nothing compared to seeing her standing here, so sure in her new body and abilities. The sunlight played over her hair and brought a fiery glint into her gray eyes, and a sensation that was more than just awe twinged below my gut. Part of me—the part most aware of how long it'd been since I'd last gotten laid—started picturing what it'd be like to feel that body under mine.

I reined that part in. I'd come out here to reassure her —in my own way—not to put a move on her. Not that I suspected Ari would welcome those sorts of advances anyway. Nothing would kill the trust I thought I'd earned faster than treating her like a conquest rather than the fellow warrior she was.

Her expression was cocky as ever, but I thought I saw a shadow of the uncertainty Freya had hinted at pass through her eyes before I answered. She might be a warrior, but this was still a strange new world for her. One with dangers she'd never imagined. Both out there and possibly within herself.

What always made me feel better in the face of unknown dangers was showing myself how easily I could crush them, at least the outside ones.

"I thought you might enjoy a little target practice, of a sort," I said, and hefted the weapon I'd been carrying at my side. "How would you like to give Mjolnir a try?"

Ari's eyes widened as she took in the broad gleaming shape. "Your hammer. Isn't it enchanted or something? *Can* I even use it?"

"There's no magic on it that says who can or can't do what with it," I said. "But it is magic. Always hits its mark. Always comes right back to you. Very satisfying to play with."

That eager gleam came back into her eyes. Oh, yes, I'd picked the right offering. "Okay," she said. "You first. I want to see what I have to beat."

I guffawed and rolled my shoulder. "Let's see. The end of that low branch there on the elm." I pointed, flipped the hammer by its short handle—showing off, maybe a little—and hurled it.

Mjolnir streaked through the air and smashed into the end of the branch with a burst of splintered wood and shredded leaves. The breeze warbled around the hammer as it flew back to smack into my waiting palm. A wash of satisfaction passed through me.

"I try not to destroy anything *too* large," I said. "Or Freya gets a little testy about the landscaping."

Ari laughed. "I bet. Give me a try."

I passed the hammer to her with only a little twinge as it left my grasp. It was true that anyone *could* use Mjolnir, but it felt almost like a part of me. I didn't lend it easily.

Ari's much smaller hand closer around the handle. The muscles in her arm flexed as she tested its weight. She scanned the yard and nodded to an old fence post that had long since lost the rest of the fence. "That's coming down."

She wound back and threw, gritting her teeth at the effort. Mjolnir spun, shining, and bashed the post into a shower of woodchips. Ari clapped her hands with a cry of triumph and remembered to reach out for the hammer's return at the last second. Its momentum tugged her toward me, but she just laughed again.

"All right, that is kind of fun. You want another turn?"

"Why not?"

She handed the hammer to me, and I took aim at an abandoned squirrel nest near the top of an oak. Mjolnir sent down a rain of dry leaves and twigs.

I offered the hammer back to Ari. She set her sights on a rock about as high as my knee and twice the width of my leg, protruding from the grass in the meadow beyond the trees.

"Let's see just how accurate this thing is," she said, and whipped it forward.

Mjolnir flashed, and the rock exploded with a

cracking loud enough to scatter the nearby birds. Ari gave a breathless cheer as the hammer soared back to her hands. She looked down at it as if examining the grooves in the well-worn metal. That shadow crossed her expression again.

"It seems almost wrong to enjoy destroying something that much," she said.

A knot formed in my gut. So she'd already gotten there. It'd taken a long time before I'd ever been able to put that vague discomfort into words.

"It was only a rock," I said. "And it's practice for going up against the things that would destroy us if we let them."

"True." She raised her head. "I guess you've fought a lot of battles with this."

"It wasn't made just for bashing branches," I agreed, studying her face.

"How many people—and monsters, or whatever—do you figure you've killed?"

What was she looking for from me? I wished I had Baldur's skill at sensing emotion, figuring out the perfect reassurance. The best I could do was be straight-forward and honest, which was what I was best at anyway.

"No one in a good long while," I said. "But before that? More than a few. Always to protect my people and yours. It's what I do." I paused. "The wargs last night—those were your first kills."

She shrugged. "I mean, other than spiders or whatever. But I guess that's what I do now too. As a valkyrie. *Something* got the ones you sent before. Something is holding Odin. If it's me or them..."

133

"You'll do what you have to do," I supplied. "But that doesn't mean you have to enjoy it all the way through. I'm not going to lie. When I'm caught up in the battle rage, knowing I'm defending those who need me, it can be pretty exhilarating. I like that feeling when I'm in the moment—that power. But after the battles are over, I can't say I ever look back on those times fondly."

Sometimes I even wished the rage wasn't quite so all-consuming. But maybe I wouldn't be the defender I was without it. I wasn't going to try to sacrifice that power just to find out.

Ari glanced at me. Whatever she'd been looking for, I got the sense she'd found it.

"I saw someone die in front of me, a long time ago," she said. "Someone who probably wouldn't have, if *I'd* done what I should have done then. It was awful."

She might have meant to say more, but her voice choked up. She smiled tightly and handed Mjolnir back to me. I took it from her slim fingers, and without thinking let myself wrap my other hand around hers. *A long time ago.* How old could she have been then? But I could see the guilt twisted through her as plainly as if it'd been a rope bound around her body. I didn't know the exact right words to loosen it, but I could try.

"I'm sure you did everything you knew how to back then. Just like you fought with everything you had last night. No matter what happens, you're not going to let us down, Ari. Just being here is more than we should have asked of you. And I can already tell you're going to do so much more."

Her fingers curled around my palm, soft but strong,

and squeezed back. Then she pulled her hand away with her more usual smile, the pain I'd glimpsed disappearing back behind that fiercely unshakeable expression I was used to.

"And when I get back, I still have to make good on that promise to drink you under the table," she said. "So let's get on with this. No one can argue whether I'm ready to go for Odin now, right? Just point me in the right direction, and I'll find your Allfather."

15

Aria

We were supposed to gather in the living room, but I caught Hod in the upstairs hall after the others had already gone down. I took a breath to say his name, and he stopped just at that, his head turning toward me. His dark green eyes settled on my face, almost as if he really were meeting my gaze now. I wasn't sure if I'd have been able to tell he couldn't see me if I hadn't known to look for the subtlest signs.

"I wanted to talk to you, just for a minute, before we do this," I said.

"What's on your mind, valkyrie?" he said in that flat voice of his. As if I really believed he was that dispassionate after the emotion I'd seen in him the other day in the study. "Having cold feet?"

I grimaced at him, even though he couldn't see that

either. "No. I just wanted to ask..." I paused. He might not be dispassionate, but that didn't mean he'd be compassionate either. I couldn't think of any better way to put this. "The last three valkyries didn't come back. I plan on making this time different, but if I can't—if something happens, and I don't make it—would you check on my brother? At least once?"

He knew where Petey lived. As far as I could tell, he was the only one who even knew Petey existed. The dark god had been *at least* compassionate enough not to rat on me to the others about my sneaky late-night trip.

Surprise flickered across Hod's chiseled face. "I'm not going to *intervene*," he started.

"I know," I said, cutting him off. "I get it. But the idea was that after all this is over, I'd get to watch over him a little. I'll feel better knowing that someone will be there, whatever way you can be."

I intended to do a lot more than just watch if I had the chance, but we didn't need to get into that.

Hod turned his face away from me, his eyes going even more distant than they'd looked before. "What are you worried will happen to him?" he asked. "That man who was yelling at him—has he hurt your brother before?"

"No," I said, "but that doesn't mean— There are tons of things, okay? All kinds of awful things that already happen or could." Memories flickered up from my own childhood: Mom's hoarse ranting, insults that cut deep, the slam of a door, a hungry gnawing in my belly. And the worst of them, the one thing I hoped more than anything Petey never had to experience: the creak of a bedroom door in the middle of the night, the weight of a body that wouldn't take no for an answer.

My skin crawled. I pushed those memories back down where I kept them bottled. "And I couldn't fix most of those things even when I was alive, not properly. He just shouldn't be alone. Okay?"

My throat had gotten tight. Hod slid his blind gaze toward me again. "All right," he said gruffly. "He won't be."

Relief rushed through me. "Thank you," I said. "Really. It means a lot to me."

"I know," Hod said. "That's why I agreed. Now go on. Valhalla is waiting for you."

I was pretty sure Valhalla had no interest in me at all. The gods had made it clear I wasn't a typical upstandingly moral specimen who should have *deserved* all the powers I'd gotten. But oh well. The Hall of Heroes would just have to deal with me sullying up the place a little on my way through.

When we reached the huge living room where I'd first arrived in the house, the other gods were ready. They'd cleared a span of the hardwood floor. Loki motioned me into the middle of that space, and the five divine figures formed a circle around me.

"Unlike us, normally a valkyrie would be able to find her way straight back to Valhalla in Asgard from the human realm without any help at all," the trickster god said. "Lucky for you, it's tied to your nature, no bridges or paths required."

"But I can't take any of you with me?" I said. That would have made this quest a hell of a lot easier.

"Unfortunately not," Loki said, his tone turning wry. "Unless, I suppose, you harvested our souls as chosen warriors, but that skill was only meant for human mortals, and it would require our dying to test it out. So we're not especially keen to give it a shot, seeing as failure may be permanent."

"Fair enough. So, how do I make this happen?"

"Since *you've* never been there before, the matter is a little muddied. So we'll stick with what's worked before. We'll all picture the great hall in our minds. You use your special valkyrie sensitivities to absorb that sense of it. That should trigger a recognition inside you to open up the way. All you have to do then is follow it."

"And then once I'm up there, I'll see some sign of where Odin's gotten to?"

Loki nodded. "Your valkyrie nature is bound to him just as it is to Valhalla. Once you're there in his hall, you should feel a sort of call leading you to the right door to whatever realm he's in. Go through, observe enough that you can give us a decent sense of where that is, but get out of there as soon as you're in any danger. Which may be quite quickly, given the disappearance of the others, so be on guard from the start."

"Bring a weapon," Thor put in. "The hall is full of them. You'll have your pick."

"And then to get back here...?" I said.

"Picture this house and open one of the Midgard doors," Baldur said in a bright tone that smoothed a few of the jitters out of my nerves. "It will take you straight back to us." He sounded as if he were sure I'd make it that far.

I dragged in a breath. It was one thing to find I'd been turned into some kind of mythical being with wings sprouting out of my back. Now I was about to leave Earth —or at least the human part of it—behind completely, to leap off into who-knew-what. My hand dropped to my pocket to trace the line of my switchblade.

I'd just have to be ready for anything.

"Good luck," Freya said, her voice wry, but when I glanced at her she smiled with a lot more warmth. Of course she did. They all wanted me to succeed. This was the whole reason they'd summoned me in the first place.

Lucky for them, I was just as keen on getting this job done as they were. They had their home and someone they cared about on the line, and so did I. It didn't really matter that mine were totally different, did it?

I squared my shoulders and drew my back up straight. "All right. Let's do this."

In their circle around me, the gods closed their eyes, remembering Odin's hall behind those eyelids. I took another breath and closed mine too so I could focus completely on the impressions they gave off beyond sight, beyond sound.

A sense of warmth and a sharper flickering heat washed over me, and an image formed in my own mind of a great hearth. Joyous shouts, an atmosphere buzzing with mead and good humor. Brilliant light reflecting off gold on the walls. A huge expanse full of boisterous companionship and—

A thread of connection twanged deep inside me like a string on a guitar. I was meant to be there. That place was meant for me. My pulse stuttered, but I grasped hold of the thread without hesitation. Grasped and yanked myself forward along it.

My body shook, and the air warbled around me. The bottom of my stomach dropped out. Then I was stumbling onto my hands and knees on a polished oak floor.

Bright light shone all around me. The floor was smooth and dry, but a faintly alcoholic odor wafted off it. All that mead, absorbed from thousands of spills, I guessed.

I eased myself upright. The shakiness seeped out of my body, leaving only a weirdly comforting feeling as if I'd finally gotten home, even though I'd never been in this place before.

Valhalla had changed a lot since the memories the gods had used to guide me here. The huge hearth still lay at the far end, but no fire roared in it now. Rows of long oak tables filled the space beneath the high arched ceiling, but the benches all stood empty. The whole place was silent except for the whisper of my feet over the floor as I moved. The gold plating on the walls still gleamed brightly, but even it looked kind of melancholy.

No more honorable warriors. No more valkyries. No more anyone, from the looks of it. I rubbed my arms, chilled by the vast emptiness even though the air was warm.

The weapons Thor had mentioned were mounted on the lower walls—spears and swords and axes of all sizes, some tarnished, some glinting as if freshly polished. As I studied them, something balked inside me.

Those weren't my kinds of weapons. I wouldn't feel

comfortable with any of them in my hands. Not like I would with my switchblade. It'd been enough when I'd taken on the wargs.

Loki had picked me for this job because he wanted someone different, someone who didn't fit the usual valkyrie mode. So I should keep being that. I palmed my switchblade from my pocket and swiveled on my feet.

Light spilled not just through the many windows but also a wide door opposite the hearth. The rest of Asgard, the world of the gods, must wait out there. Curiosity tickled at me, but that wasn't what I was here for. I was here to find Odin.

My gaze fell on an immense gold throne next to the hearth. I'd never met the ancient god who was lord of the valkyries, but I could almost picture him sitting there, leaning forward as he took in the crowd with a knowing smile on his weathered face, silver glinting amid the brown of his hair and beard.

The image sent another twang through me, softer but deeper than the call of Valhalla. Odin was out there, somewhere beyond these walls. I was meant to be his champion.

I followed that tug down the hall all the way to the throne and hearth. Standing at the edge of the huge fireplace, I could make out a doorway beyond the dead embers. I picked my way through the ashes and pushed it open.

My breath caught. On the other side, a branching path spilled out over a chasm so deep the bottom was swallowed in shadows. The silence in the dim light felt even more ominous than in the hall behind me.

I eased forward to the start of the path and realized it was branching in a more literal way. The surface of the path was roughly ridged like bark. The whole thing was an enormous tree laid on its side, its branches splitting off into the thicker darkness.

The trembling thread inside me urged me onward. One of those branches led to Odin.

I treaded carefully onto the trunk, not letting myself look into the chasm. The main path, at least, was several feet wide. I stayed in the middle and watched my balance. My wings might save me if I toppled over the edge, but who knew in this crazy place? I unfurled them over me.

One, two, three, four branches passed before the call to Odin tugged me to one on the left. The branch was only a few feet wide, the chasm even darker as I ventured across it. A door came into focus at the end. I would have been relieved if I hadn't been so uncertain about what might be waiting beyond it. But I wasn't exactly sad to leave behind this creepy place.

I flicked out my blade and braced myself with my other hand on the doorknob. Slowly, I turned it, all my heightened senses on alert.

Nothing showed itself on the other side of the door except a darkness so thick it was solid black. I didn't have any choice. I had to go through.

Folding my wings close to my back, I stepped over the threshold.

The blackness hit my body like the cold smack of an ocean wave, and then I was through. My feet hit rough rocky ground. Cool damp air closed around me along with a thinner darkness broken by a faint gleam of light far ahead of me. A putrid smell like rotting meat reached my nose.

I registered that in the first split-second, and then a mass of figures jumped at me from all sides.

My street-honed instincts might have been all that saved me. I ducked and rolled in an instant, lashing out with my knife and my foot at the same time. Bodies collided over me with hoarse breaths and jabbing elbows and a blade slicing through my shoulder to the bone. The jolt of pain flared through all my senses.

There was no room for fair play in a brawl. It was me or them. I shoved myself up with my wings, my knee ramming into what felt like a groin, switchblade whipping through the air, fingers jabbing where I thought I caught a glimpse of eyes. Go for the soft bits. Hit wherever you can cause the most pain.

My knife struck its mark, hot blood spurting over my hand. I flung myself away as some kind of spiked club slammed into my gut. Fresh pain of my own sparked all through my abdomen. A grunt burst from my lips. Another attacker flung itself at me, and another.

I spun and kicked and jabbed, pulling on all the god-given strength I had in me. My elbow smashed into something round—a skull?—with a sickening crunch. A sharp edge scraped across my shin. My leg wobbled, and I heaved myself away again, toward the light. They were coming at me too fast for me to get a real hold on any of them, to wrench away one or another's life with the darkness inside me as well as my blade. If I could at least see...

The putrid smell thickened. In the dim light, my frantic gaze caught on a row of symbols cut into the rock wall, twisted lines melded together into deformed shapes. Then it found two bodies slumped by the wall up ahead —not attackers I'd taken down. Human corpses that looked as if they'd just been tossed there haphazardly, the red ring around one's neck suggesting she'd been strangled. My stomach lurched just as shrieks that sounded equally human echoed from around the bend where the light was.

I didn't have time to decide whether continuing that way was the best idea. My attackers hurtled after me, shouting in a language I didn't recognize but could grasp the shape of: They were calling for help.

I dodged, but one had already smashed one of my wings with his club, clinging on for another blow. A second rammed his head at my already bleeding gut. I cried out as the first wrenched at my wing, but I managed to stumble far enough that the blow to my stomach only clipped my side. A ram of my knee cracked that figure's collarbone.

Five more attackers came running from around the bend, all of them like the ones I was still struggling with: limp black hair plastered against sallow skin, eyes so pale the irises blended into the whites, bodies short and stout in stained tunics and short pants.

Pain was already radiating through every part of my body. Odin was somewhere here, but I couldn't get to him. I didn't even know if I could fend off the attackers already on me.

Valhalla. I had to get back to Valhalla.

I punched at the guy on my wing right through the flesh and feathers, sending more agony splintering through its surface but knocking him off into the wall at the same time. My switchblade slashed across another's face. I hurled myself backward, away from them and the others rushing to join the skirmish, as fast as I could.

Valhalla. Valhalla. Through the haze in my head I focused on my memory of that lonely gold-drenched hall. The thread of it vibrated inside me. I clung on and hauled with all my might.

The caves and my attackers warbled away. I sprawled out of the darkness onto the polished floor. Blood streaked the floorboards as I shoved myself into a sitting position. Pain seared deeper into my gut. Cuts throbbed on every limb. I didn't think I could count on my valkyrie skills to heal me from injuries quite this deep.

I stared at the arched ceiling. Valhalla wasn't good enough. I didn't just need to be here. I needed to be home.

Midgard. Baldur had said something about doors.

My ankle wobbled under me when I tried to push myself onto my feet. Sprained, at least. I dragged myself closer to the walls.

There. Doors, a few of them, scattered between the windows and the weapons. If I could just make it to the nearest one...

I propelled my battered body along, gritting my teeth against the stabs of agony, ignoring the trail of blood I was leaving in my wake. I'd said I'd make it back. I'd said it, and I was damn well going to do it. No pack of shrimpy soulless demons was going to get the better of Ari Watson.

I had to grope upward two times before my fingers closed around the doorknob. They clutched it and wrenched.

The door flew open into a vast blank space as bright and blue as the summer sky. I closed my eyes, thought of the soft green lawn outside the gods' house, and shoved myself over the threshold.

My body thumped into the grass, which wasn't quite as soft as I'd been hoping. A strangled sound shot up my throat. I rolled over, and then I couldn't seem to move at all. Pain weighed me down like a heap of boulders. I was buried in it.

"Ari!" someone shouted. Thor, I thought. Footsteps thumped across the yard. I frowned up at the stark blue sky.

"They didn't get me," I announced raggedly to whoever happened to be listening. "I didn't let them get me."

Then darkness swam up over my vision, and I tumbled down into a void inside my head.

16

Ari

Baldur's gentle hands lingered on my stomach. His godly magic had repaired my wounds while I'd been out of it, but prickles of pain remained here and there. I had the feeling I'd taken some damage that couldn't be patched up that easily, even by him. His softly handsome face was briefly solemn as he concentrated.

Where he touched me, I could feel a glimmer of what had to be his life energy, warm and bright as sunlit gold. Just as the gods' emotions were almost undetectable to my new senses, I'd never noticed any of their living essences before, even though I could pick up on people from miles away. Even close like this, the hungry void in me didn't stir at all. Apparently no valkyrie could claim a god's life. I'd just have to hope I didn't meet any I had a reason to fear.

Really, all I could do was lie back on my bed where I'd woken up an hour or so ago and let Baldur do his thing. And, you know, try not to think about the fact that I was lying half-naked on a bed with one of the most gorgeous men I'd ever known putting his hands all over me. I wasn't usually guy-crazy, not even a little, but everyone has their limits.

Baldur leaned closer to inspect my shoulder, bringing warmth and a scent like a breeze through spring fields. I studied the ceiling, but I got a twinge down low anyway.

Okay, as soon as I was done with the whole valkyrie-on-a-mission thing, I had a few things of my own to take care of. Number one: going to see Petey again. Number two: getting this damn itch scratched with the nearest halfway decent non-godly man.

A little voice in the back of my head reminded me of all those myths about gods cavorting with mortals. It wasn't impossible that one of the four here might be up for a hook-up. I just had trouble seeing that as a good idea. I was tied to them enough without making things that much more complicated.

Anyway, before I worried about *any* of that, we had other problems to take care of.

"So, what happens now?" I asked. "Those... people, or whatever they were, that attacked me—what are we going to do about them?"

"Dark elves," Baldur said helpfully. "From what you said, you found yourself in Nidavillir, their realm."

Elves, huh? I'd have expected those to be smaller and pointier eared, but what did I know?

"Okay, dark elves. They've got to have Odin if my

sense of him led me there, right? And from the way they came at me, they must have been guarding that entrance. I guess we know what happened to the other valkyries. I also saw those dead humans there—it sounded like the dark elves were hurting other people too, torturing them or something. We're going to go after them, aren't we?" Pay them back for all the shit they'd put me and who knew who else through.

Baldur nodded, straightening up. "We now have a much better sense of direction. We can't reach Nidavillir through Asgard as you did, but the lower realms connect in other ways. There should be a few entrances we can access from Midgard. For now we'll keep watch for dark elves coming and going in your world, and in time they should lead us to one of those."

In time. I grimaced. I'd like to bash around those bastards with Thor's hammer right now—or watch him do it, which would also be acceptable. They'd practically killed me all over again. If I hadn't been able to tell that from the agony I'd been in stumbling back here, I'd have known for sure from the look on Thor's face when I'd woken up. He hadn't been sure I *would* wake up.

He'd been worried about me. Possibly they all had. Even Hod had looked a little relieved when I'd started talking, although he might just be glad he didn't have to fulfill the promise he'd made me.

"I can help with that," I said, squirming into a sitting position. My body felt stiff, like I'd overdone it with a workout a day ago, but the last of the sharper pains were gone. "How do we find dark elves?"

"Hey." Baldur's lips curved with a smile. "You did

what we asked of you, even though it was clearly a difficult fight. You've earned some rest, Aria."

I didn't feel like resting. Every time I closed my eyes, I saw those sprawled human corpses in the cave, heard those desperate shrieks. Whatever the dark elves were doing, I didn't think Odin was the only one in trouble.

"How am I supposed to rest with those freaks running around in *my* world?" I asked. "We've got to stop them."

"We will," Baldur said. "We'll take every step we can. You've already played the most important part you could."

He hardly even sounded fazed. He'd just found out that the leader of the gods, his father, was being held captive by a bunch of weirdo elves that were going around trying to slaughter anyone who interfered, and he might as well have been talking about a day at the beach. I frowned, studying his face as he stood up beside the bed.

"Are you really that calm all the time?" I said. "Doesn't *anything* bother you?"

I thought I caught the slightest twitch of a muscle in his temple. Enough to make me want to peel back that dreamy exterior and find out just what made up the man underneath. I *knew* there was more to him than he showed.

Then Baldur shrugged and gave me that same sunny smile. "This is just my nature. No matter what happens, the sun shines down on us. We'll find our way through. I trust in that, so no, I don't worry."

"Oh, yeah? You weren't even worried when everyone

was *dying* and the world seemed like it was going to hell during Ragnarok?" I was improvising a little, but I'd gotten the gist of it from what the other gods had told me.

The light god's dreamy expression definitely shifted then. Just for a second, a brief tightening, but his voice came out a little strained too.

"I wasn't there for Ragnarok. I couldn't feel anything about it."

He glided out of the room as if he were a beam of light before I could ask him anything more about that. I blinked at the doorway he'd disappeared through. Guilt pinched my stomach for provoking that reaction, but it was followed by a deeper pinch of curiosity.

He hadn't been there? Then where the hell had he been?

Somewhere he wasn't too happy remembering, from the looks of things.

Well, that was another mystery for another day, if he ever wanted to speak to me again. Today, I had some dark elves to take on. No way was I going to be able to relax just lying here in bed waiting for someone else to get things done.

I eased myself gingerly to the edge of the mattress and found that when I stood up I only felt as if plywood splinters were jabbing through my muscles, not whole knives or anything. I'd experienced worse. Being hit by a speeding jeep put a lot of things in perspective.

By the time I'd made it to the hall, the splinters were more like sandpaper grit. A steady improvement. Voices carried from the second floor. I shuffled down as quickly as I could manage.

When I pushed open the door to the study, Loki, Thor, Hod, and Freya all fell silent where they were gathered together by the desk. Thor opened his mouth, probably to ask whether I really should be walking around, so I jumped right in.

"Okay," I said. "I'm back in one piece. Where are we looking for these dark elves?"

———

The piney scent of the nearby forest hung in the air even on the downtown strip of the West Virginia city I was checking out. This high in the mountains, it was even a tiny bit cool as summer went. Goosebumps rose on my arms when the evening breeze tickled past me.

I should have brought a jacket. Of course, that would only have gotten in the way of my wings if I needed them.

The gods had said there'd been dark elf activity in this area decades ago. They weren't sure if any had been around since, but it was one place to start. I guessed they were checking out other potential leads while I poked around here.

I let my eyes sharpen as I scanned the road. Nothing had jumped out at me so far, but halfway down the main street, my gaze caught on a poster taped to a telephone poll with a photo and the word MISSING in large font across the top. I crossed the street to take a closer look.

The photo was of a middle-aged woman who looked like she'd had more hard times than easy ones. Her brown hair was scraggly and the teeth behind her smile crooked. Apparently she'd been last seen a couple towns over nearly a year ago. From the yellowing of the paper, I guessed it had been there quite a while too.

I breathed in deeply, testing the air the way I had periodically since I'd gotten here. A couple times, I'd thought I'd picked up a hint of that rotten smell I'd noticed in the cave, but as soon as I'd tried to follow it, it had vanished into the breeze. Maybe it'd just been my imagination. Or a butcher shop's trash bin. Hod had said that scent wasn't anything they usually associated with dark elves anyway.

As I continued past the shops and restaurants, a twisted shadow on the side of one building snagged my attention. I hustled closer and frowned. Three jagged lines, twined together, had been carved into one of the bricks on... I stepped back and checked the sign. It was a backpacker's hostel.

An uneasy prickle ran over my skin when I dropped my gaze back to the symbol. I hadn't had time to commit them to memory very solidly, but I was pretty sure I'd seen a marking like that on the wall of the dark elves' cave. Or at least one a lot like it.

But then, even if it had been made by dark elves, there was no way of telling how long ago or whether they'd been here since. The edges of the carving were worn down by the weather. It wasn't recent.

The prickling sensation stayed with me the rest of the way down the main street. I glanced over my shoulder abruptly a few times, but I didn't catch any movements that looked suspicious. My fingers curled around my switchblade, closed but ready if I needed it.

Around a corner in the fringes of the downtown strip, I spotted another of those symbols, this one with four lines instead of three. I paused, cocking my head as I studied it. Nothing about it meant anything to me, other than that association with the dark elves. But I didn't like it.

That one was on a small charity building. Soup kitchen and beds for the "needy." I bit my lip. No, I didn't like this at all.

Something rustled at the edges of my hearing. I stiffened, my hackles rising. The sound stopped too.

Carefully, I walked on, setting my feet as quietly as I could. Cars and other pedestrians passed me, but the street wasn't all that busy on a weekday in this nowhere town. In the gaps in between, I kept my ears perked.

There wasn't much, but the rustling reached me twice more, ever so faintly, only for an instant. That was enough.

Someone—or some*thing*—was stalking me.

17

Loki

I slunk from shadow to shadow, my wolfish shape blending into the dark patches with a mix of stealth and magic. I only caught glimpses of Ari now and then in the gaps between the buildings, but I didn't need more than that. My raised ears could pick up the soft rasp of her shoes against the pavement, even the murmur of her breath.

I did like the glimpses I caught, though. Our valkyrie was certainly coming into her own. She moved down the sidewalk with a bold but not reckless confidence it was hard not to admire.

Every time I saw it, I remembered that first moment she'd reappeared on the lawn yesterday afternoon. Battered and bleeding, she'd managed to pull herself all the way back to us—and to crow about her victory before those injuries had completely caught up with her. Then back on her feet, chomping at the bit to get moving the very next day...

I'd forgotten mortals could possess that kind of strength and fire. I didn't see it very often even among the gods. It made me want to push her even farther to find her limits and to hide her away so no one could ever batter that spirit right out of her, both at the same time.

That was all right. I was used to having complicated impulses. We'd see which one won out.

Ari's pixie frame ducked down an alley between a clothing store and a bank. Had she seen something down this way? I went still, tasting the air through my fangs. Nothing unexpected reached me. I pulled back behind a dumpster before she emerged into the longer alley I'd been loping along.

Her shoes scuffed against the damp concrete as if she were heading in the opposite direction. I waited several seconds before slipping out from my shelter to keep pace.

I'd only taken two steps when she whirled and sprang toward me with a burst of supernatural speed.

Her switchblade flashed. Her eyes widened at the sight of me. I reared back a moment before she reached me, returning to my usual form so she didn't try to kill me like the smallish warg she'd probably taken me for.

"Imagine running into you here," I said. "What a lovely coincidence."

Ari's legs had locked. Her eyes narrowed. "Coincidence my ass. What the hell are you doing here?"

I gestured lazily with one hand. "Oh, taking the lay of the land, investigating various avenues."

She crossed her arms. "*I* was supposed to be the one

investigating this town. You could have told me you were coming along. But you didn't want me to know. You were following me. You *still* don't think I can handle myself after yesterday?"

Her voice was tart, but under the snark I thought I detected a note of hurt. I hadn't realized I might wound more than her pride. And even the pride, she'd rightly earned.

My mind tripped through a hundred possible excuses to settle on the right one. "Not at all, pixie. Believe me, there's little I'm surer of at this point than your capabilities." The truth of that statement sank in as I said it. I really hadn't been worried about her, had I? I'd told myself that was why I was keeping an eye on her, but really...

I gave her a self-deprecating grin. A little more honesty couldn't hurt. "I was actually rather curious to see what other tricks you might pull out of your metaphorical hat. Watching you is leagues more entertaining than spending time with any of those lunks whose company I've already kept for eons."

Ari kept frowning, but her shoulders came down. "You aren't supposed to be entertaining yourself," she said. "We're supposed to be tracking down those dark elves."

"I'm very skilled at multitasking," I said. At her skeptical look, I nodded to the alley. "They've been here more recently than we were already aware. I've picked up traces of their passage. Not in the last few years, though, and I don't think for very long. The signs would suggest they came and went from west of here."

"Oh. Did you see any more of their symbols?"

I raised my eyebrows. "Symbols?"

She studied me for a second. When she seemed to come to the conclusion that I honestly didn't know what she was talking about, a triumphant glint lit in her eyes. "Come on," she said. "Apparently it's a good thing you weren't investigating on your own."

I followed her back onto the street and down the block. The passers-by drifted around us, not seeing us but instinctively making room. I'd have loved to see their expressions if they'd gotten to witness our valkyrie in her full winged glory. My gaze lingered on the taut muscles of her back, the smooth skin that hid those wings at the moment.

Mostly smooth. Baldur had healed her wounds from her two battles with us, but she'd come to us with other scars already in place. A thin curving one veered from the peak of her left shoulder down the back of her arm halfway to her elbow, like a path just waiting to be traced.

"There." Ari pointed to a brick in the side of a dreary-looking building. Some sort of symbol had indeed been carved there: four lines twisting around each other in a barbed tangle. My brow furrowed.

"What makes you think this has anything to do with the dark elves?"

"I told you I saw markings on the walls of that cave. I'm pretty sure this was one of them. Or at least it looks a lot like them." She paused, glancing up at me. "You haven't seen anything like this before."

I shook my head. "I'm familiar with the language of the dark elves, spoken and written, but this is something else. If you saw it in their domain, though... It's been a long time since we've crossed paths with them. If they're up to something nefarious, as all evidence indicates they are, I wouldn't put it past them to have developed some new visual code precisely to avoid our notice."

Which was not an encouraging sign at all. This building had nothing to do with Odin. What other schemes were the cave-dwellers up to that they were working so hard to hide from us?

Perhaps taking Odin hadn't been the point. Perhaps he'd merely been a casualty of a larger plot—one he'd stumbled onto?

"It's a charity for the homeless," Ari said, tipping her head toward the building. "I saw another symbol on the hostel a couple streets over. No others so far."

I turned that information over in my head. "Ports for people far from home or without a home at all. People unlikely to be quickly missed."

Ari's jaw tightened. "That's what I thought too. But what would they want with people anyway? Why would they be hurting—killing—humans? Do they have something against *us*?"

She still said "us" so easily, as if she weren't so much more than mortal now. Bristling as if she were preparing to defend the entire human race.

"I don't know," I said. "It's not their standard modus operandi. But whatever ghastly business they're into, we'll uncover it and put a stop to it—you can be sure of that."

She nodded, turning on her heel, and her gaze jerked

to the side. I'd caught a flicker of dark movement by one of the roofs too. "What was that?" Ari muttered, and before I had a chance to answer, she was already dashing toward it.

"Whoa there." I caught her by the waist—not roughly, but with just enough force to stop her. She'd put so much energy into her dash that the interrupted momentum sent her stumbling back against me. Her shoulders collided with my chest. My arm instinctively eased around her, my head dipping next to hers. "Always in such a rush, pixie."

She shoved out of the loose embrace and spun around with a ragged breath, still close enough that its warmth grazed my throat. Behind the already fading flash of panic in her dilated eyes, there was a shadow of desire. The sight of it went straight to my cock.

Our valkyrie didn't like to be held, but some part of her craved my touch.

"Why did you stop me?" she demanded.

I reined in my own cravings, the ones I'd been trying to ignore now stirring more insistently inside me. "You're quick to race in, no fearful hesitation," I said. "It's commendable. No one would ever mistake you for a coward. But sometimes slow and careful gets the job done better."

"I can be *careful*," she bit out. Her eyes were still stormy. She closed them for a second, swallowing audibly. "Maybe I'm a little wound up because of what I saw in those caves. Thinking about what those *things* might be doing to people—people who have no one to fight for them..." She looked at me again. "But you said you believed I can handle myself. I'm not going to do anything stupid."

"I know," I said. "I do." Faced with that unwavering gaze, I was run through with a piercing sensation from gut to breastbone.

I'd brought her to this place, in more ways than one. I'd ripped her out of the blank peace of death to fight battles for gods she hadn't even known existed. More than anyone, I should know the strain of being forced to play by rules I hadn't agreed to. Perhaps I owed her a little more.

"If I interfere, it's not about you," I said. "It's about me, and how much is riding on us finding Odin. Getting back to Asgard."

"What do you mean?"

I sighed. "My powers are fading faster than the others' are. And every attempt we make at finding the Allfather that fails, you can be sure they're more and more inclined to blame me. I'd rather not deal with that. All right? If I micromanage, you can attribute it to that. It's certainly no failing on your part."

Ari wet her lips, holding my gaze. "Why would they blame *you*? You picked me, but the other valkyries—"

I shrugged, letting a smile creep across my face. "What can I say? I'm a trouble-maker. So it's easy to blame all possible trouble in the world on me."

Her expression tensed for a moment, as if she could relate to that idea more than I would have guessed. "So you picked another trouble-maker to have on your side."

My smile grew. "I suppose you could look at it that

way. Although we'll have to see whether you decide to be on my side after all."

She looked as if she might have had some snappy answer to that remark, but at the same moment, the dark flicker we'd seen earlier solidified into a bird. A raven. Which glided down from the rooftop it had hopped along and shifted into the shape of a young woman, her hair and eyes and the loose dress she wore as dark as her former feathers. None of the mortals blinked as she ambled toward us. They couldn't see her either.

Well, well, well. What a surprise, and yet perfectly fitting.

Ari's knife hand came up, her shoulders braced. I touched one lightly. "It's all right. At least, no immediate threat. She ought to be a friend."

The valkyrie stayed tensed. It would seem she didn't entirely trust *me* to have an accurate take on any given threat.

"Loki," the woman said in a voice that was sweet but slightly hoarse. "I've been looking for you."

"I'm not generally all that difficult to find if you're really trying," I said. "Assuming I don't mind you finding me. I almost didn't recognize you, Muninn. It's been a long time."

The raven woman gave me a smile that recalled the angles of her beak. How many decades—or maybe even centuries—had it been since Odin had returned from one of his wanderings without his usual feathered companions? He'd never bothered to explain why they'd parted ways, beyond "It was time for them to seek something more," in his typical cryptic manner. What had his former pets been up to since then?

"It has been a while," Muninn agreed. No doubt she knew the exact date and time we'd last been in each other's company. I'd never seen her shift into human form before now, but it didn't surprise me that she could. We all changed with the tides of time—and Odin's ravens had been human enough in their affect.

"Allow me to introduce Muninn," I said to Ari with a sweep of my arm. "Mistress of memory and once one of Odin's regular companions." It certainly was interesting that she'd resurfaced now. I looked back to the raven woman. "Was there any particular reason you were looking for me?"

She'd cocked her head in eerily bird-like fashion at Ari. "You got yourself a valkyrie," she said. "Fascinating."

Ari bristled, but I knew she didn't need any help from me here. "About as fascinating as a raven that can turn into a woman, I guess," she said.

Muninn simply blinked at her. "I'd imagine you're here for the same reason I am." She turned back to me. "I had a sense something unpleasant had happened to Odin. I've searched for him across Midgard but found no trace. Asgard is closed to me without his help, but he hasn't heeded my call. All of which I find rather concerning. Don't you?"

"We do," I said. "He isn't in Asgard; I can confirm that much. I don't suppose you've gleaned any clues as to his whereabouts?"

"Not so far," she said. "But I wanted to offer my help, if you're searching as well. We always did find that two heads were better than one." She smiled faintly as her halfhearted joke.

"Where is Huginn these days?" I asked. Her partner, the raven of thought, had been gone just as long.

She shook her head. "He went off on his own adventures. Eager to spread his wings, you might say. We haven't spoken in a long time."

Her demeanor suggested nothing but concern and a little wistfulness, and Odin's ravens had been nothing but loyal in the centuries they had been in our midst. I never trusted anyone or anything completely, but we might as well make use of her offer.

"What have you seen of the dark elves?" I asked, and gestured to the carving on the wall. "Or symbols of theirs like these, here in Midgard? They seem to be tangled up in the matter somehow."

"I saw those marks in their caves, too," Ari put in.

Muninn frowned, studying the marks. "The dark elves hadn't caught my attention, but I can think of a few places we should explore."

18

Ari

"You saw dark elves around this end of town recently?" Hod asked as we walked through a shabby neighborhood on the outskirts of Pittsburgh.

Muninn, who was leading the way, nodded. With her sharply pointed chin, the movement reminded me even more of the raven I'd watched her transform into and out of a few times now. It was more unsettling than Loki's various shifts. At least he still moved completely like a man when he looked like one.

"I don't remember exactly when," she said, her voice a weird mixture of rough and chirpy. "But it was in the last year. And those symbols you've pointed out—I came back yesterday to make sure they were the same ones. That's what I can show you now."

Thor swung his hammer in an easy arc at his side. He'd detached it from his belt the second we'd arrived by our various magical or winged means. "If there are any dirt-eaters here now, they'll regret sticking around."

Loki cut a glance toward the brawny god. "If there are any here now, we want to *capture* them so we can question them about the entrance to their realm. Not bash their heads in, satisfying as that might be."

He said it lightly, like he said just about everything, but the memory of yesterday's conversation lingered in my mind: his seriousness when he'd admitted how much finding Odin mattered to him. It'd disappeared behind his usual joking façade a moment later, but the emotion in his words had resonated right through my heart. Remembering, I had the urge to step closer to him.

Or maybe that was just a baser part of me, remembering the feel of his arm around my body.

"We don't know yet how involved the dark elves might be in Odin's disappearance," Baldur pointed out, bringing me back to the present.

"They tore up Ari," Thor grumbled. "They're up to no good one way or another. That's all I need to know."

"I think this may be one rare case where you can't find the good in a situation," Freya said, raising an eyebrow at the god of light.

Baldur chuckled in his dreamy way. "Finding out what they know about Odin would be good, regardless."

"*If* we find them," I said. So far I hadn't seen any sign of anything supernatural in this rundown suburb. It was the middle of the day, but the clouds that had covered the sky this morning had dimmed the sun so much it felt like dusk. No sign of rain yet, though. Just muggy heat so thick you could practically carve it.

"We're almost there." Muninn picked up her pace, her steps springy as she crossed the street. Halfway down the next block, she veered toward a bungalow that was even shabbier than its neighbors. The glass in one window had been broken, only shards poking from the frame. Half of one of the concrete front steps had crumbled.

Five twisted lines marked the house's cinderblock base.

Muninn nudged the door, and it swung open with a squeal of its hinges. My skin prickled. I already didn't like the vibe of this place. It reminded me too much of houses and apartments I'd passed through during my first couple years on the street, before I'd gotten enough of a foothold to steer clear completely.

The room on the other side confirmed my suspicions. On the cracked linoleum floor between the scruffy armchairs, multicolored vials lay in a heap. A yellowed syringe sat on some smudged newspapers. The stink of old urine, chemical-laced smoke, and mildew assaulted me. I wrinkled my nose, edging around a frayed blanket stained with who-knew-what.

"Crack house," I said to the gods who'd filed in behind me. Hod was grimacing, and even Baldur looked a little ill. If I hadn't already been sure the dark elves were targeting the people least likely to be noticed missing, I would be now.

Freya edged farther into the room and toed a crumpled take-out box. "It doesn't look as if *anyone* has been here in quite some time," she said. "Look at the dust."

She was right. A thin layer of dust had collected on all the furniture, even the floor, disturbed only now by our feet.

"That's weird," I said, looking around. "The place is still open. There's even—" I prodded a deflated baggie with my toe. "They didn't completely finish their drugs. But it doesn't look like there was a raid either." I'd witnessed one of those, briefly, during a mad scramble out a window and down a fire escape. This place was a mess, but it was a mess that was orderly by druggie standards, not the total chaos of a bunch of police officers having barged through. The house should have been boarded up if it'd been identified.

"What do you think that means?" Thor asked, coming up beside me.

"I don't know." I swiped my hand across my mouth, not wanting to say what I was thinking. But what was the point in denying it? "Maybe *all* of the people who were using this place were taken away, just not by cops."

Thor let out a growl. "Are you *sure* I can't bash at least a few of them?" he said to Loki.

The trickster god was eyeing the room with vague curiosity. "As much as I respect those who live along the fringes of society, this looks like the home of the absolute dregs," he said. "I'm not sure whatever the dark elves did to them was any worse than they were doing to themselves." His voice was matter-of-fact, but the usual gleam in his eyes had dimmed. He wasn't anywhere near as unaffected as he was pretending.

"That doesn't mean they deserved it," Thor snapped. His face flushed red.

169

Loki shot him a mild glance. "Of course not," he said. "I'm just pointing out that you might want to moderate your fury, or you'll run out before we're even halfway to the bottom of this."

Thor muttered something that sounded insulting under his breath, but he let go of the argument.

"Well, there's clearly no one here, human or elf, now," Hod said. "If there's nothing else useful to do in this place, can we move on?"

Loki strode into the rooms that branched off from the first. "No secret elfy entrances, no more symbols, no clues that I can see," he announced as he returned.

"I'd hardly call that a thorough job," Thor said. He marched past the trickster god to make a check of his own.

Freya waved her hand in front of her nose. "While he's doing that, can the rest of us leave?"

"There's another spot," Muninn assured us, her eyes darting downward apologetically. "Closer to where I saw the elves themselves before. I hope we'll find out more there."

After we'd been waiting on the tiny patchy lawn for a few minutes, Thor stomped back out, his expression grim.

"This way!" Muninn said, darting on down the street.

I fell into step beside the thunder god as we all trailed after her. I'd never seen him this upset before. And it was over a bunch of junkies.

But if I'd had just a little less luck in those first years after I left home, I could have ended up in their place.

They were still people. People the dark elves were going to have to learn to steer clear of.

"You really care about them," I said. "Everyone the dark elves might have hurt. Don't you?"

Thor heaved a breath and looked at me. His face still had that angry flush. "I'm the god of men. I'm supposed to protect your entire realm. I can't do much about what you do to each other, as much as it pains me sometimes, but I should at least be able to stop other beings from preying on you. How long has this been going on without my even noticing?"

He wasn't just angry with the elves. He was angry with himself. The most powerful man I'd ever met felt powerless right now.

A little ache ran through me. I had the urge to take his hand, whatever comfort that was going to give him.

Oh, why the hell not? It didn't have to mean much. He'd been there for me, and I didn't doubt he would be again—as long as we had the same goals, at least.

I reached for his hand and slipped my fingers between his much thicker ones, giving them a quick squeeze. A twitch passed through Thor's muscles. A hint of the bright golden energy I'd felt from Baldur yesterday tingled over my skin. I guessed that was just what the life of a god felt like.

Thor squeezed my hand back, as gently as I suspected he was capable of, which was still pretty firmly. My heart jumped at the brief sensation of being pinned in place but steadied out the instant he relaxed his grip.

"Ari," he said, so low and tender my pulse thumped for a totally different reason.

"Here!" Muninn called out from ahead of us. "This is the other place."

Thor's jaw tensed. I let my hand slide from his as he hurried to join Muninn. Whatever he'd been going to say, he could say it later. Right now, I was really hoping he'd get to bash some dark elf skulls after all.

The building Muninn pointed to was an elementary school. My hackles went up as we approached. Were these assholes taking *kids*? Hell yes, skulls definitely needed to be broken then.

I saw the symbol right away, scratched into the concrete frame around the main doors. This one looked more recent to my eyes than the others had, which I guessed fit what the raven woman had said about the dark elves being here not long ago.

It was a Saturday, so the building was dark. Loki motioned toward the lock, and the doors eased open. We all tramped inside.

Our feet echoed loudly in the empty hall. Every school smelled the same, didn't it? Like photocopied paper and cheap glue.

A lump filled the bottom of my throat. It was too long since I'd seen Petey, since I'd really talked to him. I wanted the dark elves dealt with, but he came first. The next time I could slip away for a few hours, I was out of here.

Freya peered into one of the classrooms we passed. "I suppose we should search the entire building for any signs?"

"Or we follow this." Hod stopped, rubbing his shoe against the floor with a rasp. A fine gray grit dappled the floor in a faint splotch. The kind of grit that might be left from someone passing by who'd been wandering in caves not long ago.

Thor strode forward. "There's more this way," he said.

We hustled after him around a bend in the hall and through a set of double doors that opened into a gymnasium. This part of the school smelled like old sweaty socks. I swiveled in the dim light, searching the floor and then the walls. "Why would they come in—"

The bleachers next to us erupted with a flurry of movement. Pale-faced black-haired forms hurled themselves toward us with glints of blades. A yelp of warning, too late, broke from my throat.

Thor roared and swung his hammer. I fumbled for my switchblade. One of the dark elves slammed into me, knocking me to the floor. I jerked to the side as he stabbed at my chest. Wings. I needed my wings.

They erupted from my back with a force that shoved me, swaying, back onto my feet. Two more of the dark elves sprang at me. They were all around us, a wave of them, filling the air with the scent of damp mossy rock.

And blood. I leapt into the air, managing to kick off the elf that wrenched at one of my wings, and caught sight of Muninn ducking with a thin cry as an attacker sliced his knife across her arm. Thor pummeled several with his hammer, but another threw herself at his shoulders, sinking her knife into the muscles there. Streaks of red splattered the gym floor.

Baldur pushed back a few with a brilliant burst of light. Hod was whipping shadow around him, but not quickly enough to stop a dark elf that ducked under them and jabbed at his calf. Loki had shifted into his wolfish form. He snarled and lunged at the nearest attackers, but a gleam of blood already smeared his dark gray fur. A golden falcon soared down to claw at another elf that stabbed at him. Was that Freya?

The power and skill the gods were fighting with took my breath away. But there were too many of the dark elves, another darting in as soon as one fell back, swarming the bunch of us in a raging mass.

I swooped down, kneeing the one clinging to Thor's back in the face, lashing out with my switchblade at the clump that had surrounded Muninn. In the instant they fell back, she sprang into the air with a burst of feathers, raven again. Behind me, someone let out a hiss of pain. The elves raised their voices in a battle cry as if they were already victorious.

No. I couldn't let this happen. I was a fucking valkyrie. The one real purpose I had was turning the tide of a battle. And I needed a tide that was going to sweep these miscreants all the way back to the wretched caves where they belonged.

Another dark elf flung himself at me, and as I dodged him, a second flung himself off another's back to ram his knife at my head. I elbowed him away only fast enough to stop the knife from outright entering my skull. It scraped across my scalp, his knuckles colliding with my forehead in a burst of pain.

I tried to summon the blast of lightning I'd flung at the warg a few days ago, but my body wouldn't comply. Apparently I needed to be panicked completely out of my mind for that to activate. But I had other methods of destruction.

The flame of darkness inside me unwound through my body as I spun around. It yawned with an unsettling hunger that I was more than happy to give into. I swept out my arms, slicing one elf across the gut and digging my fingers into another's lank hair.

The pulse of the creature's life energy beat against my palm—and flowed up into it. The darkness loomed and swallowed, and the dark elf collapsed. I'd taken his life in the space of a second.

A painful exhilaration filled my chest. An attacker raked her dagger across my wing, but I battered her aside with a punch and wrenched myself back out of the fray. But only for an instant. I dove, smacking my palm against the scalp of an elf breaking through Baldur's golden shield. Snatching at another who was ramming his blade at Hod's side. The darkness inside me opened its maw wider, inhaling one life and another.

I couldn't reach them all, but I reached enough to shift the tide. As one, two, three more bodies fell in my wake, Thor let out another roar and charged through the mass of attackers. His hammer toppled at least half a dozen more. Loki leapt into the space he'd opened up, tearing throats open with his wolfish claws and teeth.

Another cry went up among the elves, but this one sounded desperate. In a blink, those still standing bolted for the bleachers. Thor barreled after them, his face nearly as deep a red as his hair, his eyes wide with fury. His hammer slammed through several more. Loki pounced on another with a rake of his jaws. Muninn shot down from above and jabbed her beak into a fleeing elf's neck.

"Baldur!" Freya called. She was standing with Hod, who'd fallen to his knees. Blood was soaking down the dark god's slacks from a wound at his waist.

"No," he gritted out. "I'm fine."

She merely scoffed. His bright twin rushed to his side. I sank to the ground myself, the throbbing of my own injuries catching up with me. A sharp ache dug into my temple. My scored wing crackled with pain.

Fallen dark elves sprawled all around us, none of them moving. Thor came to a stop, his chest heaving, the flush starting to fade from his face. "I don't know where the rest of them disappeared to," he growled.

We hadn't managed to catch any to question. We'd been too busy not dying. But Loki just grimaced, swiping a hand at his own wounds. "For now, I'll say good riddance."

We'd won the battle. And now we knew a little more. It wasn't just Odin the dark elves had a beef with, clearly. They'd have happily killed all of us—and they'd come way too close for comfort.

19

Ari

When I woke up from the nap Baldur had induced while I healed, the sky outside my bedroom window was dim but not dark. Pale pink streaked across the clouds from the setting sun. I focused on that pretty color for a moment as echoes of the battle with the dark elves rose in the back of my head. The blood. The battering. The heady sensation of the life energy I'd wrenched from their bodies.

My stomach rolled. I shook the memories away. Like Thor had said when we'd talked about fighting, I'd been defending myself and people who needed it. One slip, and it'd have been my life destroyed all over again. It wasn't as if I'd *wanted* all that violence.

Right now, there was only one person I wanted to be thinking about. One person I should be thinking about.

I crawled out of bed, testing my limbs to make sure

they were all back in working order. If I'd felt like I was recovering from an intense workout after my first confrontation with the dark elves, now I was coming out of a rotten flu as well. I grimaced at the burn in my muscles and went out into the hall.

It was still early enough that I could make it home before Petey's bedtime. I had to actually talk to him this time. Let him know I was here, that I was still looking out for him. I sure as hell couldn't go into another battle without doing that.

No voices sounded from below. The house was still and silent, only one light on downstairs—in the kitchen. A thick savory smell greeted me when I walked in. A note was lying on the table.

Dear pixie,

Thor insists we let you keep sleeping, and I have a feeling I'll end up with his hammer in my head if I argue any more. We're checking a possible lead. There's stew in the fridge if you're hungry, and Hod is probably in the study being grim if you have any use for him. I promise we'll save some dark elves for your blade.

He hadn't signed it, but the spiky handwriting would have told me Loki had left it if the nickname and the jaunty tone hadn't.

I might have been annoyed, but their leaving without me had made my life that much easier. I had only one god to worry about, and conveniently the one I had some hope of making a case with. I yanked open the fridge, bypassed the stew—as good as it smelled—for a more portable bun I stuffed a few slices of ham in, and headed for the study.

"Yes?" Hod said when I knocked on the door. I pushed it open to find him sitting at the desk where he'd been the last time I'd visited him in here, only this time he had a book open in front of him. His hand lay flat against it, but as far as I could tell it didn't have any braille. He'd been using that magical way of reading he'd hinted at before, I guessed.

His unseeing gaze had lifted toward me. "What is it, valkyrie?" he asked.

Of course he knew it was me. No one else was here. For all I knew, he could tell from the sound of my breath or the rustle of my clothes. Not much seemed to get past him, regardless of his blindness.

"I thought I should give you a heads up," I said, "so you don't have to chase me down again. I'm going to see my brother. I won't be gone too long."

Hod frowned. "I don't think—"

"I'm going," I said firmly. "I did everything you all have asked me to do—and more—and now I'm going to do something for me. Unless you want to fight about it."

I wasn't sure how much of a fight I could really make against a fully-fledged god. Hod didn't look particularly worried. He sighed and rubbed his temple, scattering the fall of his short black hair along his forehead.

"All right," he said. "But you're not going alone."

I bristled as he stood up. "You still don't trust me?"

He managed to give me a glower. "Mostly I don't trust the dark elves and whoever they might be allied with. But no, I don't entirely trust you either. The whole reason Loki picked you is because you look out for yourself first. Or am I wrong and you're actually selflessly devoted to making the world a better place?"

Now I was *really* bristling. "You don't have to be an asshole about it," I said. But there wasn't a whole lot else I could say. The truth was I'd already planned on breaking at least one rule in the next couple hours. And it wasn't like I had any intention of sticking around and doing my divine duty after we got this whole dark elf problem sorted out.

That wasn't selfishness, though. I was thinking of Petey at least as much as myself.

"Are we going or not?" was all Hod said.

I muttered something highly insulting under my breath and marched to the front door, trying to pretend I didn't feel him following behind me.

On the front lawn, I tugged forth my wings. They sprang from my back with hardly a prickle now, as easily as my knife from the switchblade handle. Like they were becoming even more a part of me instead of some alien appendages tacked on.

I didn't totally like that idea, but there was no denying they were useful. With a few quick flaps, I was soaring toward Philly. Hod careened along behind me on his shadowy magic carpet.

I wanted to lose myself in the rush of the wind and the flow of the landscape beneath me, but anxiety had balled tight in my gut. I'd gotten too distracted by the dark elves and the horrors I'd witnessed in their realm. It didn't matter how many people they might be preying on —Petey had to come first. He needed me more than anyone. I'd promised him I'd be there for him.

But for now, he was still dozens of miles distant. There wasn't much to distract me except the god of darkness skimming along beside me.

"Why did they leave you behind anyway?" I called over to him.

Hod kept his face turned forward, as if he were navigating by sight. "I was the most injured in the skirmish this afternoon. They assumed I needed the most rest."

The same reasoning they'd used with me. I guessed I couldn't be too offended if they'd treated one of their fellow gods the same way.

"Are you *sure* you should be flying all this way, then?" I asked. "I'm telling you, I'll be perfectly fine on my own."

He shifted his eyes toward me then, the green even darker in the deepening evening. "That didn't work back at the house," he said. "It's not going to work here."

I shrugged with the sweep of my wings as if it didn't make that much difference to me. "Well, you can't blame a girl for trying." Another, more unnerving question nibbled at me. "Do you really think we need to worry about the dark elves out here?"

"What do you mean?"

"You're the one who mentioned them, and they did hit us pretty hard today. If we hadn't all been together..." I paused. "Loki said you all can still die. And that you don't know if you'd come back again if you do."

Hod made a dismissive sound. "Loki says a lot of things. I'll admit those things are true, but we're a lot more resilient than any mortal. The dirt-eaters had the upper hand, briefly, because they caught us by surprise and we weren't expecting an assault. We won't make that mistake again."

That didn't mean they couldn't surprise us in some other way. But I shook off that uneasy itch, pushing my wings faster as Philly's city lights came into view up ahead. The sense of home loosened the clenching in my gut a little. My valkyrie senses could even pick up the hum of all those human lives ahead of us, breathing and eating and laughing and all the things humans were supposed to do.

I could still do all those things as a valkyrie. Just not with other human beings, if the gods had their way.

I glided over the rooftops until I reached Mom's street. Then I swooped down in a perfect arc to land on Petey's windowsill.

He was crouched on the bedroom floor, making gruff voices for his action figures as they waged war across his thready rug. His head didn't even twitch when I settled on the ledge by the half-open window.

I just sat there for a few minutes, watching my little brother at play. His gray-blue eyes were bright but distant as he focused on his imaginary world. Whatever story he'd cooked up, it involved half the contents of his toy bin —although he didn't exactly have a huge number of playthings anyway. A lock of over-long blond hair fell into his face, and my fingers itched with the urge to brush it back.

This part was going to require some quick thinking— and acting. I didn't glance over at Hod, but I could feel him hovering a few feet away, waiting. I wasn't getting him to leave, even for a minute. That was obvious. So I'd just have to count on my speed and his sense of discretion.

Petey made one of his superheroes blast off into the air. I gripped the window ledge and focused all my attention on my body: the muggy but cooling evening air against my skin, the flaky paint beneath my palms. At the same time, I yanked my wings back into my body.

"Valkyrie!" Hod said, and I knew I'd done it. I shoved myself through the window's opening an instant before his grasping hand whipped through the air behind me, just missing my arm.

My feet thumped on the floor, and I winced. But I was in, breathing the sour scent of the sheets Mom never bothered to wash in the warm room. Petey spun around. A grin leapt across his face, so joyful it made every painful moment of the last week completely worth it.

"Ari!" he whispered, knowing he had to stay quiet even in his excitement. He sprang off the floor and threw his arms around me, pressing his face into my shoulder as I crouched into the hug. The sweet smell of childish skin replaced the room's less pleasant odors.

My pulse hitched. Petey's embrace felt different from usual—more desperate.

"Hey," I said softly, running my hand over his rumpled hair. "Is something the matter?"

"Mom said I wasn't ever going to see you again," he mumbled into my shirt. "I *knew* she couldn't be right."

Those two sentences told me all I needed to know. Mom had found out about my death—and she'd decided she could cut deeper by making Petey think I'd abandoned him than by telling him the truth.

I hugged my little brother tighter. Too bad for her I had ways of coming back and proving her wrong.

Knuckles rapped against the window. When Petey didn't flinch, I realized only I could hear them. As I'd hoped, Hod was staying unperceivable. He couldn't come in here and drag me away from Petey without causing a whole lot more distress.

The god of darkness could be cold, but he was also logical. And his sense of logic should be telling him letting me play normal with Petey for a few minutes would do less harm than trying to intervene.

"Valkyrie, get out of there," Hod growled, but I ignored him. I squeezed Petey once more and kissed his cheek. As I eased back, the collar of his shoulder slipped to the side and revealed a mottled purple-and-brown mark just above his collarbone.

My pulse stuttered. "Petey, what happened to you?"

My brother's eyes went wide. "It's nothing," he said quickly. "I tripped and fell."

A twist of rage and guilt wound around my stomach. "Let me see," I said, keeping my voice gentle.

Petey stiffened, but he held still while I shifted his shirt even more to the side. His narrow shoulder—goddamnit, why didn't Mom give him more to eat?—held not one but four splotchy bruises, like fat splayed fingers. Tripped and fell, my ass. My own fingers clenched around the fabric of his shirt, careful not to brush the tender skin.

"Ivan or Mom?" I said, already pretty sure of the

answer. Mom dealt in neglect and willful obliviousness, with a side of emotional torture. She'd only raised her hand at me once, and that had been the day I'd left. But she had a taste for violent men that even seeing her first son dead hadn't cured her of.

Petey's his lower lip wobbled. I forced my hand to relax and patted his arm. "It's okay, buddy. You can tell me. I won't get you in any trouble."

"I knocked his favorite mug off the counter, and it broke," he mumbled. "It was an accident."

"Of course it was. He's just... He's just a big bully." I swallowed all the coarser names I'd like to have called him and tugged Petey to me again. The darkness that had stirred in the battle with the elves this morning was churning in my belly. Somehow it made me feel both queasy and invincible at the same time.

I didn't want my little brother seeing those feelings in me. Didn't want him catching even a glimpse of what his Ari was capable of now.

"I can't stay," I said. He was used to that. "I just had to see you. I'll *always* be around, watching out for you, even if you don't see me for a while. Okay? And next time I'll bring a pack of those cards."

I waggled my eyebrows at him, and his smile came back. He couldn't feel it—the fury radiating through my veins. I ruffled his hair one last time and straightened up.

"I love you, Ari," he said in his innocent six-year-old way.

"I love you too, kid," I said, but my throat tightened. He hardly knew who I was anymore. *I* hardly knew that.

But I knew what I could do, and I knew exactly who I had to do it to.

By the time I pushed myself back out through the window, my body was shaking. Hod clamped his hand around my forearm, and the effort I'd been making to keep myself visible dissolved.

"What in Hel's name was that?" he snapped.

"Get off me!" I shoved him away, jerking my arm out of his grasp, and dove with my wings surging out over my back. I could hear the TV going in the basement. Ivan would be down there in his stupid little man cave. Pathetic fucking man who'd smack around a little kid. My anger seared through me, burning dark and deep. The rest of the world around me faded amid that roar.

He was never going to touch my brother again.

"Ari!"

Hod tackled me from behind as a wall of his shadowy magic slammed into me from the other side. We both crashed into the lawn, just a few feet from the basement window I'd been aiming for. I hissed and lashed out at him with elbows and knees, but the dark god pressed me into the earth with his hands and tendrils of shadow.

"Let me *go*," I said, outright flailing now. "He deserves it. He deserves every bit of hell I can rain down on him. Fucking bastard."

"Ari." Hod's voice was low but strained. "This isn't your place. You can't just go around killing random people because you're angry."

"He's not a random person. He's the asshole who hurt my little brother. Get the fuck off me!"

"I'm not going to," Hod said. "Not until I know

you're listening. And I've got more power in one hand than you've got in your whole body, valkyrie, so don't try me."

I gritted my teeth. "I *have* to do this. You don't understand."

Hod's eyes gazed down at me, flat and yet fathomless at the same time. "Then why don't you tell me about it?"

I dragged in a breath—every muscle quaking at the sensation of being pinned down, all that fury and pain and guilt writhing inside me—and burst into tears.

Hod flinched and leapt back. The shadows clinging to my legs loosened. I slapped my hands to my face, but they couldn't hold in the tears or the sob that wrenched up my throat. Fuck, fuck, fuck. Get a hold of yourself, Ari.

I swallowed hard and swiped at my eyes. A few tears streaked down my cheeks, but I managed to inhale without a hitch. Hod stood braced between me and the basement window, his eyes wary, his mouth twisted. Lord only knew what he was thinking now.

When he spoke, his voice was still strained, but there was a softness to it I'd never heard before. "Go ahead and tell me. I'm all ears."

The corner of my mouth twitched despite myself. My fury had spent itself with the tears. Now all I felt was an aching emptiness inside.

Had I really wanted to be a killer? I didn't know. But then, I already was one.

I'd never killed a human being before, though.

I wet my lips and drew up my knees, resting my hands on them. My gaze stayed on my dirt streaked fingers as I found the words. "It's not a very exciting story. I had a crappy mom. She liked to date crappy guys. My older brother tried to protect me, but he was practically still a kid himself."

"Your *older* brother," Hod repeated.

"Francis." It'd been years since I'd said that name out loud. It made my mouth turn dry. "He gave me that switchblade. Told me it was his way of being with me, if he ever wasn't there, if I needed it. But even when things got really bad— I didn't use it when I should have. I *gave in*. Such a fucking coward. When Francis found out, he attacked the guy. The guy attacked back, slammed his head into the corner of the kitchen counter."

I sucked in another breath. "Second-degree murder, they called it."

That was one memory I'd never be able to shake. I didn't want to. Francis deserved better than being forgotten, even that last gut-piercing moment when I'd stood over his crumpled body seeing the blood pooling beneath his pale hair, with tears blurring my vision and a shriek in my throat.

"The man who did all this," Hod said. "He's in prison now?"

He didn't ask what I'd given in to. What Francis had found out. I hadn't known I could feel as grateful as I did right then. The memories of those awful nights, pressed into my lumpy mattress, willing my mind away while that bastard grunted and pawed at me and more... I would have left *those* behind forever if I could. They wrenched at me too much even when I didn't look at them directly.

"Yeah," I said. "At least five more years before he's got

a chance at parole. But Ivan could turn out just as bad. I can't let anything happen to Petey. I can't just let things *happen*, let him get hurt because I didn't try to stop it."

My voice had gone ragged again. I shut up. We stayed there through a long stretch of silence.

"I do understand," Hod said abruptly.

My gaze jerked up to his face. He was frowning, his head bowed.

"What do you mean?" I said. How could a god have any fucking idea—

"I know what it's like," he said, "to feel like you killed someone you love." He laughed roughly. "I know it better than I'd wish on anyone. At least you— How old were you, Ari?"

My fingers dropped to the grass, twisting into the strands. "Twelve. But it doesn't matter. I still should have done more."

"You can't, though," Hod said. "It's already over. All you've got left is the rubble in the aftermath."

He said it with a hollowness that resonated with the empty ache inside me. I wanted to argue, but that statement was true, wasn't it? Even if I stole Ivan's life from his body, it wouldn't change a damned thing about what I'd done or hadn't done ten years ago.

Hod held out his hand to help me up. I hesitated and took it. His grip loosened when I was on my feet, but he eased a step closer, raising his other hand cautiously. My breath caught as he rested it on my hair just above my ear. Not close enough to be an embrace, but maybe as close as I could have accepted right now anyway. Part of me wanted to lean into him and part wanted to run away, so I just stayed where I was, in between. Held but not quite held.

"You won't let him down," the dark god said quietly. "I can tell. There'll be a way. It's just not this."

My throat choked up all over again. I blinked hard. I still didn't let myself step right to him, but I leaned my head into his touch, just a little. Taking the comfort he was trying to offer just for a moment.

The energy that whispered beneath the dark god's skin was the same golden warmth as Baldur's and Thor's had been. In that way, he and his twin were completely the same.

"I want to believe that," I said.

"Stranger things have come true for you in the last week, haven't they?"

I looked up at Hod even though I couldn't exactly meet his gaze. His mouth had quirked with a bittersweet smile.

"Come on," he said. "You're not killing anyone tonight. Let's get home."

20

Baldur

Loki had the laptop open on the dining room table, chuckling to himself as his long fingers clattered over the keys. The rest of us peered at the screen from our cluster around him. Windows of text and images flew by on the screen.

"Gods using computers," Aria said. "I'm not sure this is a good mix."

Her tone was teasing, but when I glanced at her, her face looked drawn. Was she worried about the laptop or something else? An echoing worry stirred inside my chest.

"It's an *excellent* mix," Loki declared. "My new electronically inclined friend—the one who gave me this computer, not the computer itself, as much as I adore it— set me up with some picture recognition software. In theory, it should seek out matches for those symbols the dark elves are using through all the public photographs on the internet. We'll be able to see if there's anywhere they're particularly condensed."

"And if there is, that should be where their gate from Midgard to Nidavellir is," Thor filled in.

"Exactly! No need for us to run all over the world to find it. Although I won't fault Muninn for keeping up her search that way."

"It'll only work if they were careless enough to leave signs that obvious," Hod said.

Loki waved him off. "Oh, take your gloom and doom someplace else, nephew. I have internet access. Soon I will rule the world!"

He winked at Aria, and she smiled, but there was tension in her expression that I couldn't help seeing. It sent a shiver through my nerves.

"Any tools we can use to get us closer to Odin are a blessing," I said. "I'm sure it'll come up with something useful."

"There," Loki said. "The god of light has spoken. No further argument necessary."

"Let us know when you've solved all our problems, then," my twin muttered. He turned to go, hesitated, and lifted his eyes in my direction with a motion of his hand to follow him.

I walked with him out into the hall and up the stairs. His hand skimmed the banister, a barely necessary point of orientation. His movements looked a little stiff, though.

"Are you still in pain from yesterday's attack?" I asked. "If you need me to work more healing—"

Hod shook his head with a jerk. "I'm not asking for

anything from you. Everything is perfectly healed. You don't have to worry about that."

He led the way into the study and stopped by the desk. For a moment, he just stood there, bracing his hand against the wooden surface.

"Brother," I started.

He swiveled abruptly to face me. "We've never talked about it," he said. "What happened—the mistletoe, Loki's ploy... Not really."

A chill so strong and swift I couldn't displace it swept through me. "Because we didn't need to," I said, pushing warmth into my voice and trying to let it warm the rest of me. "I know it wasn't your fault. I know you never would have meant to. There's nothing more to be said."

"There is," Hod insisted. "Allfather help me, brother, I don't know if I ever even apologized. It was so long, in between, and then after we were just glad Ragnarok was over, and I never wanted to press you. I never wanted to remind you of what you must have been through. But I know it can't have been easy for you."

"Hod," I said. "It's done. I don't think about it, ever." I didn't let myself. "You can absolve yourself."

"Can I? It was my hand. It was my doing as much as his. I know he likes to blame everything on the damned prophecies, but you never deserved a fate like that. You—"

"It's *done*," I snapped. The words crackled from my mouth as if the ice inside me had mixed with my voice. "We're in the light now. Let us stay there."

Hod winced, his whole body going rigid. A sharper agony wrenched through me. I was supposed to be here to keep the peace, to bring joy, not lose my temper when he was obviously only trying to help, as unwanted as that help was.

"Baldur," he said roughly.

I touched his arm before he could go on, summoning all the warmth and light I had in me. Letting it wash over those prickling reminders of the past and melt them away. I might have said it badly, but what I'd said to him was true. We had to focus on what we had now, where we were, and all that was good about it.

"There's nothing to apologize for," I said, "because there's nothing to forgive. We had our roles to play, and we did, and everything happened as it was supposed to happen. I promise you, I don't bear a single shred of resentment." That much, at least, was also true. "Let's think about what's ahead of us, not what's behind."

Hod paused and then nodded. "I shouldn't have disturbed you. You're right."

He sat down at the desk. I glanced around at the rows of books ranging from old to new across the shelves, and a quiver of that chill stirred inside me again. "Be peaceful," I said to my brother, and went out to chase a little more peace for myself.

The music room was my surest route. As I headed toward it, the creak of the stairs drew my attention.

Aria was climbing up from below. That discomforting aura still hung around her. My heart squeezed.

I wasn't sure I'd been able to comfort my brother all that much, but I could offer more to our valkyrie. I should, or I'd be failing her too.

I waited for her to reach me. She gave me a questioning look with a raise of her eyebrows. I nodded toward one of the doorways down the hall.

"Would you join me in the music room? I feel that perhaps we could use something to clear our heads for the challenges still ahead of us."

She inhaled sharply, and for a second I thought she was going to refuse. Then she shrugged. "Sure," she said. "It definitely can't hurt."

She trailed behind me into the room. Simply stepping inside sent a wash of calm through me. I breathed in the scents of fine wood and polished metal, and everything inside me stilled.

Yes, this was what I needed. I couldn't ease the chaos going on around us unless my own spirit was easy. And if I could make Aria's spirit rest easier too, then at least I'd have accomplished something fruitful today.

Aria cocked her head as she considered the rows of instruments. "I don't know how to play anything. I don't even know that I'm *that* great a singer, but if you really want the company..."

"You enjoy it, don't you?" I said. I'd felt the pleasure of it in her when she'd sung briefly along with my viola the other day. "That matters more than skill."

She snorted. "I guess that depends on who's listening. But okay. I don't know if we know many of the same songs, though. How up are you on the latest pop charts?"

I chuckled. Just talking with her was already setting me more at ease, before I'd even picked up an instrument. She always seemed so... impervious.

"Not the most recent ones, perhaps," I said. "But I am

intrigued by current music as much as by the classics. I may just be a few decades out of date still. Whenever we travel down to Midgard, I've always got a lot catching up to do."

"A few decades. Let's see. Why don't you tell me what music *you* like from the most modern eras you've caught up to, and we'll figure out where I can fit in."

I considered my most recent dabbling. "I have become rather fond of Liza Wang and Ahmed Rushdi, but I suppose English songs are a better bet?" Her puzzled look was enough of an answer. "I have found much to appreciate in the works of Elvis Presley, and Stevie Wonder, and The Beatles."

Aria laughed. "Seriously? All right. I can work with that." She cracked her knuckles. "I had at least three music teachers in school who were Beatles maniacs. Let's medley that up. Do you know 'Ob la di, ob la da'?"

I picked the acoustic guitar off the wall. "Well enough to manage the tune."

A glow came into Aria's face as we launched into the song, matching the glow that spread through my chest as my hands moved over the strings. There was something so pure and joyful about calling forth a beautiful melody from such a simple object. If she didn't hit every note perfectly, it didn't matter. Her voice wove through the sounds of the guitar from that song into "Can't Buy Me Love" and "Hard Day's Night."

I started picking songs somewhat at random, just to see where we could match. If she didn't pick up the thread partway through the first verse, I simply switched again. Aria grinned, caught up in the challenge.

Without thinking about it, I shifted from the more energetic songs into softer tunes. My thumb strummed the opening chords to "You've Got To Hide Your Love Away," and Aria's mouth twisted.

Her voice spilled out as sweet as before, but lower, with a slight tremble as she reached the chorus. No, this exercise had gone in completely the wrong direction.

I stilled my hand against the strings, and her voice faded out. She shook her head, running her fingers back through the messy waves of her hair.

"Sorry, we can try again."

"You were fine," I said. "You were great." Perhaps right now I needed to take a direct approach. The subtle one clearly hadn't worked well enough. "Whatever's wrong, Aria, you're with us now. We have hundreds of years of experience tackling whatever the realms throw at us. We'll see this through. It'll be all right."

She looked at me from behind her hand. "You can't know that," she said. "You don't even know what's bothering me. What if it isn't all right? Not every problem gets fixed, you know."

"Then you set those concerns aside and find other things to take joy in," I said. "Why dwell on what you can't change?"

"Because you don't know whether you can or not?" she said with a swing of her arm. "Anyway, it's not as if you can just ignore everything that makes you upset, bury it forever."

I blinked at her. That was the only thing you *could* do, often enough. "Why not?"

"Because... because it's still there. And you'd know

it's still there, even if you're not letting yourself think about it. Even if you're distracting yourself and acting like there's only the good stuff. I've tried it. It never works for very long."

Something tightened around my chest, not exactly painful but not comforting either. The comment that tumbled out wasn't one I might have said otherwise. "If you bury it deep enough, it can be gone for centuries."

Her gaze focused on me. I made myself look back at her, even though the sensation inside me had tightened even more. "It's not really gone in that case, though, is it?" she said quietly.

"It may as well be," I said. "If it never comes back up. In which case, what does it matter, if everyone's happier that way?"

"I guess I'm just not that good at burying things."

I set down the guitar beside my stool and stood up. "Then let me help you."

She held herself in place as I stepped closer to her. I raised my hands to either side of her face, just barely grazing her cheeks with my knuckles. She could sense my surface emotions just as I could sense hers. I thought of the last few days, of everything I'd seen of her, and let admiration flow from me to her.

"You found us a way back to the Allfather," I said. "You've fought for yourself and for the rest of us. You have wings to soar on and strength no mortal can match."

The corner of her lips quirked up. "I've nearly gotten myself killed twice," she said wryly. "I *did* get myself killed a couple days before that. I'm sneaky and selfish when I need to be, and if you'd met me before I became a valkyrie, you wouldn't have been complimenting me at all."

"I don't know about that," I said. "But you are a valkyrie now, even if you've been sneaky, even if you've been selfish. Because of that, really, since Loki was doing the picking. It's part of your strength."

"Right. One off-key mortal note in a symphony of godliness."

The metaphor brought a smile to my face. None of my godly companions would have made that comparison. She fit here more than she realized—more than maybe I'd realized until just now. She was a part of our harmony, twining through all our disparate melodies. I wouldn't have wanted to let that go, no matter how many other emotions she stirred up in me that I might have wished to keep buried deeper.

I opened my mouth to tell her at least part of that, and her gaze twitched away from me. Her brow furrowed.

"Aria?" I said.

"There's something—" She cut herself off, her eyes going even more distant. Her attention had shifted to something beyond this room, something I couldn't detect. In some ways, her valkyrie senses were sharper than mine.

She glanced at me briefly. "Thank you," she said. "For trying. There's something I just need to—to check." Without another word, she slipped out of the room.

21

Aria

For the first minute after I left the music room and crept down through the house, I started to think I'd imagined hearing... whatever I'd even heard. The noise had been so faint, right at the edges of what my newly honed ears could pick up—but something about it had pricked at the hairs on the back of my neck. That seemed worth investigating even if I couldn't explain why.

There it was again. I froze on the bottom step, straining my ears. The sound was barely a whisper. A shiver passed through me anyway. I needed to find it—to find out what it meant.

Loki, Thor, and Freya were still chatting in the dining room around the computer. I assumed Hod was off in his study again, his favorite spot to hole up. No one came after me when I eased open the front door. Either they were too occupied to notice me leaving, or at this point they all trusted me to at least come back.

I palmed my switchblade and flicked it open, scanning the lawn. Nothing looked out of the ordinary. If the sound had really been all that threatening, Loki at least should have noticed, right? His senses had to be even more finely tuned than mine. He was the one who'd given me that power.

I wavered, debating whether I should go ahead on my own or get back-up first, and the breeze carried the sound to me a little more clearly. It was laughter. Childish laughter from somewhere distant.

It sounded almost like *Petey*.

My shoulders tensed. That didn't make any sense. No one except the gods even knew I was here, and none of them except Hod knew Petey existed. As gentle as he'd been with me in the end last night, I didn't for a second believe the god of darkness would have brought my brother out here for a surprise visit.

I stalked across the trimmed grass through the warming mid-morning sunlight. How far away could this kid be? I skirted a couple of the trees at the edges of the main property and veered off the path when the laughter reached me again, still faint, but getting louder. I was closer.

I'd walked another few minutes when something stirred in the shadow of an old elm tree on the other side of the overgrown field I'd just reached. The laughter spilled out from there. It sounded even more familiar now. Nerves twitching, I pushed on, the long grass hissing against my pants. The plastic handle of my switchblade was dampening with sweat against my palm. But if it was a kid, I didn't want to hurt him.

"Who's there?" I called out. "Over by the tree. Can you move where I can see you?"

I was about ten steps away when the figure sidled to the edge of the shadow. Not right into the light, but close enough that I could see her features. Lank black hair, sallow skin, eerily pale eyes. A dark elf.

My legs locked. My head whipped around, but I didn't see any others of her kind nearby.

"What do you want?" I said. Was there any chance this one actually wanted to help us?

The crooked grin she gave me turned that possibility into dust. She opened her mouth and let out another peal of that laughter. Bright and high like a little boy's. The hairs on my neck stood straight up.

It *was* Petey's laugh. She was imitating it somehow, note for note.

"Ari," she said, in Petey's voice. "You wouldn't let anything bad happen to me, would you?"

My knife hand shot up, but I held myself still, as much as I wanted to charge at her.

"What did you do to him? What the fuck is this about?"

The dark elf ducked her head almost bashfully. When she spoke again, it was in a dull rasp of a voice that sounded nothing like my little brother at all.

"We haven't done anything to him... yet. If you want him to stay safe, you'll leave us alone."

I stared at her. My mind was still struggling to catch up through my initial burst of panicked anger.

How had they even figured out about Petey? Had they gotten lucky, just happened to see me head out there last night? It wasn't as if any of them could have followed me, keeping up with my wings on those stumpy little legs.

But it didn't really matter, did it? They did know, and they'd gotten close enough to him to learn the sound of his voice. They'd been willing to attack gods, to target the homeless and school children... I didn't for a second believe they'd hesitate to hurt Petey if they thought it would get them what they wanted.

"Okay," I said. "Fine. You do whatever the hell you want, and I won't say boo. Just stay away from my brother."

She held my gaze with her unearthly eyes. "You're the one who needs to stay away. Stay away from the gods you've been helping. Don't say a word of this or anything else about us to them. Go, now, and don't come back."

"*What?*" I sputtered.

She folded her arms over her chest. "We're watching. We'll know. If you set foot near that house or the gods in it again..." She bared her teeth. Jagged teeth like splintered rock.

My heart thumped. Leave the gods. It was because of them I was still around at all, not to mention I had them to thank for my powers... but I'd always intended to leave, however I could, when they'd found Odin. I was staying here on Midgard, end of story.

Bowing to her threat felt different, though. Like running away with my tail between my legs. I didn't fight battles I didn't think I could win, but I wasn't a coward either.

I didn't have much choice, did I? I'd thought it myself just yesterday: Petey came before everyone else. The dark elves could be tearing down the whole rest of the world, and it was Petey I had to protect first. I'd promised him. Just yesterday, with that trusting little face gazing up at me...

That jab of guilt in my gut—I had to bury it, for him. Bury it way deep down like Baldur had said. Bury myself way deep down where the gods couldn't or at least wouldn't be bothered to track me down.

They didn't really need me now anyway, did they? I'd pointed them at Odin's kidnappers. That was all they'd really expected of their shady valkyrie. They'd kept trying to get me to stay back at the house. Even they couldn't claim I was letting them down somehow.

The memory of yesterday's battle flashed behind my eyes. The darkness churning inside me, the lives it had sucked away. The exhilaration in those moments...

My chest clenched tight. One more thing to bury. For Petey. Everything, always for Petey.

"All right," I said. "I'm going. Don't you dare even touch him, or you'd better believe you'll regret it." I flipped the switchblade back into its handle with a little more force than was necessary.

The dark elf didn't look intimidated. She just watched me with those peeled grape eyes as I unfurled the wings from my back. I shoved off the ground, away from her, away from the gods' house.

I had to be fast, this first stretch. I didn't know how far their senses could follow me with that faint connection between us. Once I had enough distance, I could go to Petey...

My wings kept beating at the air in a swift steady rhythm, but the bottom of my stomach dropped out.

I couldn't go to Petey. That was the first place Hod would look for me, whether he could sense me or not. The dark elves weren't going to care whether I *wanted* the gods coming to me or not. They'd just see that I was talking with them again.

I propelled myself through the air even faster, the landscape below me blurring, the wind stinging my eyes. Just go. Far, far away, where they'd never think to look. Bury myself for real. Until it didn't matter anymore, until they'd won their way back to Asgard and everything in my life could go back to being—well, as normal as it could be.

———

The last of the fading sunlight burned the sky orange-brown along the horizon. The ache spreading through my wings dug a little deeper. Each flap felt more ragged.

I'd been flying for hours. I had no idea where I even was anymore, other than I'd left New York and Philly far behind. No gods had caught up with me, so I guessed I'd done all right. But my wings were about ready to collapse. It was time to come to earth.

A hum of human energy called to me from just up ahead, where city lights gleamed. The pulse of all those living bodies breathing, eating, dancing...

Yes. That's what I wanted. That was the perfect way to bury the hollow that had been spreading through my abdomen since I'd set off on this flight. One night of just pretending to be the girl I'd been a couple weeks ago—or someone even more free than her.

I dipped lower and lower as I skimmed over the suburbs and into the city proper. My feet touched the sidewalk beneath a sign lit with neon lights, and my wings folded into my back with a sound like a sigh. I walked straight into the club.

Inside, the warm air washed over me with the tang of alcohol. Strobe lights rippled over the crowd of undulating bodies. I snatched a shot off the tray of a server weaving past me and threw it back in one gulp. The sour liquid seared down my throat.

The server looked around, trying to see who'd snatched the glass. It looked like I'd be drinking free this one night. A smile stretched across my face with the tingling buzz of the alcohol. I lifted another glass and leapt on into the crowd.

The bodies parted in my wake like they never had when I'd just been another solid form in the sea. I spun and bobbed in time with the pounding music. My hair whipped against my face; my arms swayed in the air.

One song bled into another and then another. My wings had been tired, but the rest of me was ready to let loose. I grabbed a third shot, which was strong enough that it made me wince on the way down, and threw myself harder into the music. By my fourth, my head was starting to fizz. That was good. A fizzing head couldn't think about all the assorted people I'd left behind.

It wasn't quite the same, dancing like this. I liked not having to worry about some random dude grinding up against me, but at the same time, I missed the actual feeling of contact. Knocking elbows accidentally. Brushing past my fellow human beings to make room. Knowing I was there, part of the crowd, one of them.

But I wasn't one of them. Not anymore. I never would be again.

All right! Time for another shot. I snatched up a blue one this time and drained it. The glass slipped from my fingers and shattered on the floor. I stared at it for a moment, and then I stomped on the shards, letting their crinkling sound blend into the music.

I whirled one way and shimmied another, my fellow dancers shifting away whenever I came near them. The pulse in my head was almost as loud as the music. I swayed and spun—and faltered when my gaze caught on a tall lean figure slinking through the sea of bodies, straight toward me. As if he knew exactly where I was.

Because he did. The multicolored lights dappled Loki's pale red hair and paler skin. He raised an eyebrow as he reached me, his lips forming their usual sly grin.

22

Ari

Loki didn't say anything at first. He moved with the music, with a grace that shouldn't have surprised me but did here in the midst of all those mortals, sidling closer to me and then easing a little farther away. That eyebrow stayed arched as if challenging me to keep up with him.

I started to dance again in defiance of the heavy thump in my chest. Stepping even faster, whirling even tighter, hitting every beat as if I knew them by heart. Loki matched me move for move, every motion so fluid it was hard to tear my gaze away. I wanted to reach up and run my hands up the lean muscles I could see beneath his tunic, the way I might have in a different club on a different day, if a regular guy I liked the look of that much had looked at me that way.

Loki's eyes never left mine, flickering with their

amber light even here. He eased closer, setting a cautious hand on my waist as we dipped together. A flush spread over my skin at the contact. He bent his head close beside mine—close enough that suddenly I couldn't smell anything except the hot spicy-sweet smell of his body, ginger and cardamom and a dash of honey. Good enough to eat.

"If you wanted to dance, there wasn't need to cross half the country, pixie," he said by my ear. "I can even vouch for a few of the clubs right by us in Manhattan."

"Maybe I wanted a bigger change of scenery," I said.

"Hmm. I almost feel as if you were trying to escape *us*. But why could you possibly want to do that?"

A jolt of panic broke through the haze in my head. The dark elves. Would they see us even here? Would they punish me for being found?

My body went still. I pulled back far enough to meet his gaze. "Could anyone know you're here? Not just these people." I waved my hand toward the crowd. "Dark elves, or—or whatever."

Loki had stopped when I had. He stayed close, his hand still resting on my side. His eyes narrowed. "No one, human or dirt-eater or otherwise, could have followed me. What happened, Ari? Why did you run?"

My throat tightened. But I had to tell him now, didn't I? He'd found me. I didn't have any excuse I could make up that I was sure would be good enough to get him to leave without me.

"A dark elf came by the house," I said, as steadily as I could manage. "I have a little brother back in Philly. They figured that out somehow. She said they'd hurt him

—kill him—if I helped you at all again. She said they'd be watching to make sure I didn't even go anywhere near you."

Loki's jaw tightened. "Petey," he said, and then at my expression, "Hod told us about your little trips when we realized you'd disappeared. He went out there to look for you. You don't have to worry about that, pixie. When I don't want to be seen, I'm not seen. Although at the time it was mostly you I didn't want to tip off."

A little of the pressure inside me eased off. My buzz crept back in, relaxing me just enough for curiosity to take hold. "How did you find me?" I asked.

He shrugged as if it'd been no big thing. "Instinct. We all called you to us when we summoned you, but I was the one who found you that first time. I know you down to the quiver of your spirit." His lips curled up. "You could almost say we're soulmates, if you believe in that sort of garbage."

I couldn't help rolling my eyes at him, despite the wash of deeper heat those words sent through me. "The one of a gazillion soulmates who happened to die at just the right time?"

His smile turned sharper. "There, you see. You understand me exactly. Although a 'gazillion' may be a slight exaggeration."

He leaned in again, his breath grazing my cheek, and my heart skipped a beat. The throng was still dancing away all around us, but I didn't care about anything outside this little pocket of space that held him and me and the question hanging over us.

"Now that I've found you," he murmured, "how do I

convince you to come back?"

"Do you need to convince me?" I asked with more bravado than I felt. "I'm surprised you haven't already thrown me over your shoulder and carted me off."

He chuckled. "Come on now. You should be able to tell that's not my style. Just be glad it wasn't Thor who tracked you down."

"I can't go back," I said. "Not while the dark elves are watching Petey."

"I can make sure they never know you're with us," Loki said. "I'm not known as the master of disguise for nothing. You—and he—would be safe in my hands."

I made a skeptical sound. He touched my cheek with his other hand, easing back. His eyes searched mine. "I know how much you must care about him. I can see it. I've been there. Odin isn't even my brother by birth, but I gave up so much for his damned—" He cut himself off with a little shake of his head. "If there's one thing you believe, believe that we'll protect your brother. May I never return to Asgard if I'm lying."

His last words carried a crackle of energy as if they'd magically bound him to that oath. I hesitated, wanting to believe him, and yet...

"It's safer if I don't go back at all. You don't even need me. What does it matter where I am?"

"You're our valkyrie," Loki said. "You're our responsibility. And we might not *need* you at this exact moment, but you can hardly deny you've helped."

The memories I'd tried to bury stirred in the back of my head. Baldur was wrong. It wasn't that simple to get away from them.

"By killing people," I said.

"Well, I'd hardly call dark elves *people*, but..." Loki cocked his head. "Is that what's bothering you? You were only trying to make sure they didn't kill us."

I wet my lips. The hollow sensation in my gut came back, so deep and empty even the music pounding around us couldn't touch it. A truth I had managed to bury, so far I hadn't even known it was there, tickled up into my head.

"It isn't just them I've wanted to kill. I don't know if Hod told you everything—if he told you that he had to stop me from going after my mom's boyfriend last night."

"Because he'd hurt your brother."

So, Hod had spilled the beans about that too. I nodded. "I would have done it. Even if he'd been lying there helpless and asleep... I think I would have *liked* doing it. It felt almost *good*, taking life from those dark elves."

Loki brushed his fingers over my hair. The tender gesture wrenched at my heart. I wanted to lean into it, and at the same time I wanted to pull away, because he couldn't mean it. He shouldn't mean it, not for me.

"Ari, you're a valkyrie now," he said. "You're meant to dispense justice by shifting the tide of war."

"That doesn't mean I should have *fun* with it," I blurted out, my buzz loosening my tongue. "There've been so many times, so many people I might have wanted to get out of my way, when I never could— What if it's not just to turn the tide that I'll want to do it?" I swallowed hard. "Maybe someone like me isn't meant to have that kind of power. Maybe there's a good reason all those valkyries Odin used to summon were pure of heart and whatever."

Loki shook his head, his smile somehow grim and amused at the same time. "You know who you're talking to, don't you? Hello, I once orchestrated the end of the world. You're not going to convince me that you're somehow such a wretched soul you don't deserve the gifts you've received."

"That—that's different," I said, but my protest sounded weak even to me.

Loki leaned close again, his face just a hair's breadth from mine, bringing that spicy sweet scent with him. For a second, I thought he was going to kiss me. My pulse stuttered way too eagerly.

But he just spoke, the air from his lips moving against my cheek. "It should be comforting, pixie. No matter how bad you are, no matter how bad you get, you can never be the worst there is. I've already got that title in the bag."

His tone was light, flippant even, but a splinter of pain echoed from him into me at the same moment. The trickster god cared so much more than he liked to admit. Somehow that tugged at me even more than the closeness of his lips.

"Come back with me," he went on. "Come back with me and smash those bastard cave-dwellers right out of your realm. We won't let them lay one finger on your brother. Take all that darkness in you and rain it down on them."

I shivered. The words resonated more deeply than I liked to admit. My hands clenched. My tongue slipped away from me again.

"I'm scared," I said, so quietly I wasn't sure he'd even hear me. I wasn't sure I wanted him to. "I'm scared of myself, like this—of what I could do." To anyone, whether they deserved it or not. Of having to decide whether they did deserve it.

Of everything that came with being a fucking valkyrie, really.

"Good," Loki said, his voice nothing but warmth now. "*That*, not any 'goodness of heart,' is what makes the difference between you and someone unworthy. And think about it, Ari. If you're afraid, imagine how afraid the dark elves must be of you and what you can do, to make a threat like they did."

He sounded almost awed with that last remark. He saw me, he saw every dark place in me, and he was *awed*.

I was still a little dizzy with the shots I'd inhaled, and the warmth and the awe wrapped around me with an urge I couldn't quite bring myself to deny. I grasped the front of Loki's shirt with both hands and tipped my head that last tiny distance to catch his mouth with mine.

The god drew in a startled breath, and then he was kissing me back, hard and hungry. His thumb traced an arcing line across my side. Everywhere our bodies touched, heat tingled through my nerves as if he'd literally set me on fire. But what an intoxicating fire it was.

I let myself sink into him, into the hot heady sensation of his lips meeting mine, where nothing else mattered just for a moment. If he was going to give, then I'd take everything I could get.

He kissed me again, and the electricity of it set me

alight like a sparkler. A whimper crept from my throat when his mouth trailed away from mine, charting a scorching path along my jaw.

"Tell me you'll come back," he murmured beside my ear. "I'm not going to drag you. I want you to want to. We can make those bastards pay, Ari."

Yes, yes, yes. Fuck it. Who was I to argue with a god? My grip on his shirt tightened.

"I'll come," I said. "But first, I want to dance."

He chuckled and nipped my earlobe, already swaying with the beat of the music. The swivel of his hips by mine sent a fresh wave of fire through me. I gave myself over to it. If I burned, then I fucking burned.

———

Only the thinnest of dawn light was drifting through my bedroom window. I blinked at it blearily and rubbed my eyes.

My bedroom window—my bedroom in the gods' house. A now-familiar sheet was pulled up to my shoulders; my head rested on the downy pillow. A faint ache nibbled at my temple, but it wasn't that bad, really, considering how many shots I'd done in fairly quick succession. Six of them: five before Loki had shown up at the club and one after we'd started dancing again, before we'd gone back to kissing...

My heart flipped over. That was the last thing I remembered: his lips searing against mine. Had I —had *we*—?

I shifted under the sheet and felt the fabric of my clothes shift with me. The same clothes I'd been wearing last night: one of those racerback tanks and jeans. Nothing seemed out of place.

A strange mix of relief and disappointment came over me. I really preferred to be fully conscious when I got it on with anyone. And my first time with a *god*? Yeah, I'd like to remember that.

But I'd wanted him, I'd pretty much thrown myself at him, and clearly he hadn't wanted me quite as much.

Well, what had I expected? He *was* a god.

I sat up, kicking back the sheet, and the door eased open. Loki slipped inside, shut the door behind him, and ambled over to perch on the edge of the bed. His amber eyes gleamed in the faint light. Somehow that was enough to make me lose my breath.

Damn, I definitely needed to get laid somehow or other sometime soon, or I was going to turn into a total imbecile.

"Sleep well?" he asked.

"It seems that way." My gaze darted back toward the window. "Did you make sure no one could see me coming back with you?"

"The day a dark elf can see through one of my illusions is the day I curl up and die of shame," Loki said. "And I spoke to Hod while you were sleeping. He checked on your brother while he was looking for you. The boy hasn't been harmed. Hod headed back out there to keep watch for the dark elves—well, 'watching' in a metaphorical sense, at least."

I let out my breath. "I'm sure he appreciated that order," I said sarcastically.

"I didn't order him, actually, as much as I might have enjoyed doing so. He volunteered."

A pang of startled gratitude shot through me. The god of darkness had been kind enough after I'd dragged him out there the other night, but I wouldn't have expected him to go out of his way for me. Hod must have cared even more than he'd let show.

I swallowed my surprise and looked up at Loki. It figured that even first thing in the morning after running all over the country, he still looked brightly magnificent. I had to stop noticing that.

"Well, I'm back here now. I still don't know what exactly you think I'm going to do now that I'm here that'll be so helpful."

Loki smiled. "Oh, I'm sure we'll find some way to keep you busy."

His tone was jaunty, but his eyes were searching, as if he were waiting for something from me he hadn't gotten yet. I groped for the right words.

"About last night..."

"It was quite a night," he offered, his smile stretching a little farther, when I faltered.

Just spit it out, Ari. My hands balled in the sheets. "I don't actually remember the trip home, but obviously I slept alone." A question without actually asking the question.

"Yes," Loki said. "Well. In my experience across the ages, drunks make lousy bed partners."

My back tensed. A flood of heat that wasn't at all

pleasant coursed through my cheeks. "I'm sorry for making a pass, then. You don't have to worry about it happening again."

"Ari." Loki sighed and motioned to me. "Come here?"

My body balked, but the unexpected earnestness in those amber eyes melted some of my defenses. I scooted a little closer. Loki glanced at the foot of space I'd left between us with a faintly amused expression and then raised his head to meet my gaze.

"I regret that you were drunk," he said. "I don't regret anything about you being you. Make all the passes you want. Just make them while sober is all I'm asking. I have self-restraint, but I can't say I enjoy employing it all that much."

Oh. *Oh.* The heat that had surfaced in my face seeped down through the rest of my body, pooling low in my belly. The words tumbled out. "I'm sober now."

Loki grinned in that way that turned my whole body into a knot of want. "Yes, you do appear to be."

I shifted closer to him, my hand brushing his thigh. He touched my cheek and teased his fingers into my hair. My breath caught.

"This could still be a bad idea," I felt the need to point out.

Loki's smile widened. "My favorite kind."

And then our mouths collided.

I hadn't imagined the heat of his kisses in the club. That hot tingling spread through my nerves again, licking through every part of my body. The trickster god parted my lips with a skillful flick of his tongue that sent a bolt of need through me.

I pressed closer to him as our tongues twined, straddling his lap. Loki eased me into place with an encouraging sound and a hand on my hip. I arched against him. My breath stuttered at the feel of him hard beneath the fly of his slacks, aligned perfectly with my core. I wanted to do so much more than kiss this time.

Loki slid his hands up under my tank top, spreading that fiery tingling in their wake. His lips broke from mine just long enough to yank the top off of me. Then our mouths locked together again, trading air and heat as he made quick work of my bra.

He cupped my breasts, swiveling his palms to draw my nipples tighter with a shiver of the hottest of sparks. I moaned into his mouth. His slender fingers teased over the peaks and under the swell of them as if exploring every curve.

His lips and tongue teased over my jaw and down my neck. I wrenched at his tunic, and he helped me tug it off. We pressed together skin to skin, wave after wave of divine fiery warmth washing through me as he grazed his teeth against my throat. I ran my hands over the lean muscles I'd only caught a hint of before, firm and smooth and rippling at my touch.

With a slight heave, Loki tipped us over on the bed, his hips still between my legs. His weight shifted against me, and a spark of emotion that was more panic than pleasure shot through my chest. My pulse lurched.

Clamping down on that reaction, I gave his shoulder a light shove. When he eased back, I shoved again, harder. He let me flip him over with a flash of a grin before he reclaimed my mouth.

I rocked against him, able to lose myself in sensation now that I was on top and at least that little bit in control. My sex pressed against the bulge of his erection, and he groaned, kissing me even harder.

"Ari," he murmured, nipping my lower lip. Almost pleading. As if he wanted this even more than I did. He gripped my hips, bucking to meet me, and I moaned too.

I fumbled with his fly and yanked at his slacks. Apparently gods wore boxers. I tugged those down too, and his cock sprang free. Tall and slender like the man, and so hard it was fucking glorious. I licked my lips without thinking. My throat tightened—I didn't do blow jobs, there was no way that would end well—but I almost wanted to try, seeing him.

I settled for stroking the silky skin of his erection as I unzipped my jeans. Loki pushed himself up on one elbow and drew my mouth back to his. We kissed between pants for breath, getting sloppier by the moment. When I'd kicked my jeans aside, he slid his hand down my body to dip between my legs.

His fingers glided over my damp panties, and bliss flared even hotter through my core. My grip on his cock tightened. Loki gave another groan. His fingers leapt up to hook around the side of my panties. With one swift jerk, the fabric snapped.

Fuck me. I rubbed myself against his cock, my clit quivering. A whimper slipped out of me as he dipped his index finger right inside me. Our kisses were outright frantic now. But I hadn't lost my head completely.

"Do we need—" I started, and gave a rough laugh at the absurdity of the question. "Can valkyries get pregnant?"

Loki matched my laugh with a breathless chuckle of his own. "Not without a whole 'nother level of magic, pixie. You're safe from bearing any shifty trickster babies."

"In that case..."

I eased the head of his cock right down to my slit. He slid his fingers out to clutch my thigh as I lowered myself onto him. With a little arch of his hips, he filled me all the way. The head of his cock hit just the right place inside me to leave me trembling with desire.

We set a rhythm that was almost frenzied, me riding him and him rising to meet me, every pulse like a shot of blissful fire through my veins. His hands were everywhere, tracing flames everywhere they touched: caressing my breasts, stroking my ribs, angling my hips so I could take him even deeper.

Blazing pleasure spiraled up from my core through my chest. I tipped my head back, pumping harder, chasing my release. His thumb teased across my clit, over and over, and then pressed harder. And I exploded.

The flare of ecstasy rocked my body and seared through my vision. I shuddered over Loki with a cry. He kept his hand on my clit, pounding into me with a shaky sigh, and I came all over again alongside the hot gush of his release. In that instant, my body was nothing but heat and pleasure, and I believed I could burn my way through anything—and anyone.

23

Ari

We sprawled on the bed, Loki on his back and me tucked against him, his thumb stroking idly up and down my back. Just when I was wondering if that was it, if he'd gotten what he'd come for and was done now, he dipped his head to seek out my lips. The kiss wasn't as desperate as the ones before, but it still sent a lick of fire through me.

Maybe I'd better be clear about *my* expectations here.

I took a moment to catch my breath and then said, "Just so you know, I'm not looking for any kind of—I don't know—commitment or anything like that. I don't really do that anyway."

Loki guffawed and tickled the top of my head with a gentle sweep of his fingers. "So, what you're saying is, hold off on any professions of undying love?"

My gaze jerked up. "Were you planning on making one?"

His lips had curled with amusement. "That's not really my style either, pixie. I have, as you mortals put it, 'gotten around,' even more than the myths would indicate. I'm not going to assume I own you just because we enjoyed each other's company. You go chasing whoever else you take a mind to chase." His eyebrow lifted. "Perhaps I could even join you with another conquest sometime."

Two guys at the same time? Two *gods*? Because that was what my mind shot straight to: Thor's strong hands, Baldur's gentle touch, Hod's intense presence. I'd never tried a threesome before—it was a whole lot easier feeling in control with only one partner to keep track of—but the idea felt suddenly appealing. Maybe because one of those partners would potentially be the smoking hot god lying right next to me.

"Have you done that before?" I asked.

Loki waved his hand breezily. "I've done just about everything." He fell silent for a moment and then started grazing his fingertips over my hair again. "Although to tell you the truth, I haven't done much of anything in a while. It all got rather mundane. I'd forgotten how stimulating it can feel, being with someone who can keep me on my toes."

"Stimulating, huh?" I muttered.

"Were you not stimulated?" he teased. His tone turned a little more serious. "I'd never rein you in, Ari. I mean that. But just so you know where I stand, I do also hope we enjoy ourselves like this again."

"Hmm," I said noncommittally. The truth was that just the fleeting touch of his hand against my head, the warmth of his body aligned with mine, was enough that I was tempted to jump him again right now. But I wasn't sure admitting that was such a great idea. Loki was "stimulating" as fuck, but he was also a trickster through and through. There were reasons I'd tried to ignore my attraction.

We were here now though, so it seemed reasonably safe to tuck my head under his chin and drink in the spicy-sweet smell of his skin. A quiver of his living energy ran under it, that faint pulsing my valkyrie senses were finely tuned to.

Just like the other gods, his energy was brighter than any human or elf I'd run into. Bright and intense—but oddly not quite as warm as what I'd felt from all the others. When I focused on it, I could feel a sharp cool tang amid the brightness. More like bronze than gold. I frowned.

"You've gone pensive, pixie," Loki said. "What's on your mind?"

"Your... life essence or whatever. The other gods feel pretty much the same, but yours is a little different. I guess it's because they're all brothers?"

His hand stilled against my hair. Just for a second, but long enough that I knew not to believe his casual tone when he answered.

"No, it'd be because I'm not a god."

I pulled back to stare at him. "Ha ha, very funny."

No," he said smoothly. "It's true. You obviously aren't up on your mythology at all. Thor and Baldur and Hod are all Aesir, the rightful inhabitants of Asgard. I'm an interloping frost giant who just managed to make good with the guy in charge. Of course, I'm perfectly happy to accept the title of god when people feel like offering it."

"Oh." I guessed that explained a little more why there was that friction between him and the others that I'd noticed from time to time. You'd think they'd have gotten over it after all this time together.

"Are you deeply offended?" Loki asked. "You thought you'd landed a god but it turns out not quite?"

I rolled my eyes. "I don't give a shit what you call yourself. I just didn't realize."

"Good then," he said in that same a-little-too-casual tone. Then a more natural lilt came into his voice. "All different beings have their own sorts of energy. I'd imagine Freya comes across a little differently from the boys' club too—she's Vanir, not Aesir, although search me what separates the two. Humans are another thing altogether. As are valkyries."

He dipped his head, his lips brushing my temple. The fleeting kiss sent a fresh tingling through me, but my mind was already spinning off in another direction. "And dark elves would be something else too," I said.

"Well, yes. I supposed that factor would be helpful if we didn't have to be close to pick up on that energy in the first place."

I pushed myself upright. "I don't have to be close. I'm supposed to be able to hone in on the energy of a battle from just about anywhere."

An eager gleam lit in Loki's eyes. "Where are you going with this?"

My heartbeat raced faster. "I don't think I could take in the whole country, let alone the whole world, from here—but I could fly around—I could feel out where there are a bunch of dark elves all in the same place, emerging and disappearing. Like they were coming and going from this realm."

"Through the gate!" Loki scrambled off the bed and threw on his clothes in an impressive display of chaotic grace. "You can rest your wings. I can run through the sky faster than they'll take you anyway. With the amount of activity the cave-dwellers have got going on this side of the ocean, I don't think we'll need to cover the entire world. We can scour the country in an hour."

I grabbed my own clothes. My excitement mingled with trepidation. What if it didn't work, and I sent him running all over the place for nothing?

But this was what I'd come back for. I'd come back to try. And also possibly for super-hot not-quite-a-god sex.

"You going to carry me around?" I said, pulling on my borrowed linen pants. I really needed to find myself some new jeans.

"This isn't the time to worry about your dignity," the trickster said. "We can make it a piggyback ride. Come on. If we're quick, we can be back with good news before the rest of these slugs even go down for breakfast."

I hurried after him to the dormer window. My legs balked as he pushed it open. "If the dark elves see me..."

He beckoned me after him. "The illusion I put on you will stick until I take it off. No one will notice you're with me unless I let them."

"Okay, okay." I clambered out after him. He scooped

me up and settled me against his back exactly like he'd said, piggyback style. I draped my arms across his shoulders and braced my knees against his waist, and he sprang out into the air.

This was how he'd caught up with me at that club so quickly, I realized as he darted higher toward the sky. He hadn't been right behind me; he'd just been able to cross that distance so much faster than I had.

In the space of a couple of breaths, he'd already strode high enough up that the entire state sprawled beneath us. On our earlier travels, he must have held back so the rest of us could keep up.

"Anything around here?" he asked.

"First I have to figure out what I'm even looking for," I said. I'd been too busy avoiding getting killed by the dark elves—or worrying about getting Petey killed—to have paid much attention to the unique qualities of their energy. But as I breathed in, dragging up those memories, I found I could almost taste it anyway. Slower in its pulsing and a little thicker than human energy, slightly oily. I grimaced and cast out my senses.

Life thrummed all across the landscape below: scraps of it in the smaller towns, a boisterous burst from New York City up ahead, and everything in between. I caught a hint of that oilier energy here and there, but when I trained my focus on it, it either faded into the mass of human life or gave me the impression of nothing more than one or two figures. No larger fluctuations.

"I don't think the gate's here," I said.

"Then onward!"

Loki raced forward through the sky, miles falling

away behind us with each stride. We fell into a pattern: He paused, I reached out my senses, we moved on. Sometimes I didn't sense any dark elves at all; others there were only a few, like before. My hopes started to sink. Maybe they'd found some way to disguise their presence from my valkyrie awareness.

Loki stopped yet again, and I opened myself up to the energy humming below us. A town here, a city there, more cities dotted across the hilly landscape—and a patch of oily energy.

I tensed against Loki's back. He touched my calf where it rested against his thigh. "Here?"

"Wait." Just a bunch of dark elves wasn't enough. What mattered was what they were doing.

As I concentrated hard on that patch of lives, three of them winked out, one after the other, as if they'd died. A minute later, five new ones appeared seemingly out of nothingness. A smile stretched across my face.

Not out of nothingness. Out of their passage between their realm and ours.

"There," I said, pointing as I honed my focus even more closely. We were so high up that the cluster of buildings I was pointing at on the side of one of the lonelier hills looked like a tiny blotch.

Loki cackled to himself. "We've got them now."

I laughed too as he spun toward home, relief coursing through me. He'd strode past a few states when his head twitched to the side. "Look who's here."

He glided to a stop. A black feathered shape swooped over to join us. With a shiver of the air, Muninn transformed into her human body, other than two much larger black wings she flapped to keep herself level with us.

"Where are you coming from, Loki?" she asked, looking only at him. "You look awfully pleased. Did you learn something?"

"Only the exact location of the dark elves' gate," Loki said with a grin. "We'll have Odin back by dinnertime."

Her eyes widened. "Where is it?"

"Back hills of Kentucky. I'm about to round up the gang for a closer investigation. I assume you'll join us?"

"Of course," she said.

I adjusted my position against Loki's back, and her gaze never left his face. Understanding hit me. She couldn't even see me. Loki's illusion hid me from her, too.

"I may have a few weapons I can bring to the battle," the raven woman went on with a dark glint in her eyes. "Let me retrieve them and I'll meet up with you as soon as I can."

Loki bobbed his head to her, and she contracted back into her raven form. With a few swift flaps of her wings, she'd soared away from us.

As Loki set off again, an uneasy sensation settled in my gut. "So, we're going straight to that gate—to go through it, to fight the dark elves and get Odin back?" I said.

"That seems the obvious course of action," Loki agreed. "What's the matter, pixie?"

"Your illusion can stop them from seeing me. But if I'm fighting with you, if I'm killing them like a valkyrie—they'll know I'm there."

And then they'd come after Petey like they'd threatened.

"You don't have to make this your fight too," Loki said.

He meant that, just like the others had meant it when they'd said I could hang back before. But it didn't feel like the right answer any more than it had then.

"Even if you get Odin, it's not like you'll have stopped the dark elves from being in Midgard, right?"

"That's true. We can't exactly justify—or carry out—a total extermination. We might be able to banish them from this realm if we can find evidence of their exact crimes, and once we have Odin's powers with us again..."

"But that will take time," I filled in. "Even if they don't know for sure I helped you again, for all I know they'd kill Petey just out of spite."

Loki was silent for a moment. "I won't deny that's possible, Ari," he said.

I let out a pained breath. "Then what am I supposed to do? As long as they know where to find him, they could hurt him whenever they wanted. They might have *already* hurt him for all I know."

"No," Loki said firmly, cutting off my spiral of panic. "Hod is guarding him. He can take on plenty of dark elves himself—and if they'd made an attempt, he'd have sounded the alarm."

Right. I sucked in a breath. I owed the blind god a whole lot of thanks the next time I saw him. But still...

"I can't expect you all to keep protecting Petey forever," I said. "Or even for very much longer. You'll all have to be there to fight the dark elves off at the gate, won't you? And then you'll be going back to Asgard."

"And so will you," Loki said gently, as if I needed the reminder. But even if I could have evaded the gods somehow, convinced them to let me stay here in the human realm, I couldn't protect Petey from the dark elves' vengeance all on my own either. That knowledge sank like a boulder in my gut.

"I can't leave him there," I said. "He'll never really be safe." He never had been, even when it had just been my mom and her revolving door of asshole boyfriends. And I couldn't very well take Petey with me anywhere, could I?

I swallowed hard. Loki touched my leg again as we glided down over the house. "I think you already have your answer. We'll move your brother somewhere the dark elves won't be able to find him. And then you can show those dirt-eaters what a valkyrie's real rage can look like."

24

Hod

Ari's hair rustled as she bowed her head. Across the street, three sets of footsteps went up the front walk of a house. The sun was warm, baking the shingles of the roof we were perched on, and the breeze brought the bright scent of daffodils from the garden below, but none of that shifted the cool shadow that hung over the valkyrie.

A childish voice carried up to us. "What are we doing here?"

"We're meeting your new family," Baldur said with his calm warmth.

Ari let out a shuddering breath. "Is this really the only way we could have done this?" she said quietly.

I knew she already knew the answer to that. "If I'd left his memories, he would have slipped up. Said something that tipped people off that the story we gave them wasn't right. He could have ended up back with your mother. Even an adult who knows the full gravity of a situation has trouble living a conscious lie."

"Yeah." She drew her legs up in front of her. The feathers of her wings, still spread at her back, fluttered faintly in the breeze. "I always thought someday I'd have a proper job, a house, everything set up so I could challenge Mom for custody and win..."

"You couldn't have given him that, not the way you are now."

"Not as a valkyrie. I know." She exhaled raggedly. "I just keep reminding myself that this is better than if I'd just died and not been here at all to do at least this much for him."

The emotion in those words brought a little ache into my chest. I'd known Ari loved her brother from the first moment she'd talked about him, but love could so often be possessive, even selfish. Instead of clinging to him, she'd given up her place in his life for his own good.

"You're doing the right thing," I said. "You're looking after him the best way you could have. He's lucky he had a sister like you."

Her next breath sounded choked. Her hand whispered across her cheeks. Swiping away tears, I realized. The ache inside me bit deeper. The urge to take her in my arms had been growing in me since the first moment we'd laid out this plan to her, to pull her to me like I hadn't dared to the other night—but I'd been able to tell then that she wouldn't have wanted that. How could I say now was any different? The last thing I wanted was to remind her of the man who'd hurt her.

So I stayed where I was.

The three figures across the street had reached the house's front door. One of them—probably Loki—knocked. A moment later, the door opened.

"Oh," the woman who'd answered it said a little breathlessly. "You're here. Hello. It's so good to meet you."

"May we come in?" Loki said in a voice as smooth as usual but higher pitched. The trickster had transformed himself into a refined lady for this role—supposedly a social worker from the local child services agency. We'd picked out a family waiting for a foster child that had seemed like the best possible fit for Ari's brother, and Loki had doctored all the necessary records. Baldur was coming along as his assistant, to conduct good vibes and ease the transition.

My job, as always, had been spreading the darkness. I'd wiped every identifying memory from the little boy's head. I'd wiped all memory of him from all the minds in the city that held it: the mother who'd left him to be assaulted, the boyfriend who'd done the assaulting, the dark elves who'd been lurking in threat, the teachers and friends who might have asked after him. None of them would think to look for him now.

I couldn't have reached every single dark elf who might have been in on that threat, but we'd whisked him away to a city in Canada where Loki's computer hadn't found any signs of their activity. The chances of them stumbling on him by accident and recognizing him were slim.

He was safe. And he had no idea he'd ever had a

sister, let alone one who'd been willing to sacrifice so much for him.

"I'm fine," Ari said abruptly. Her voice didn't sound teary anymore.

"I know you are," I said, because I had the feeling that was what she needed to hear. And I didn't really doubt that she would be fine. She was awfully resilient in all sorts of ways, this valkyrie of ours.

The door to the house opened and closed again. Only two sets of footsteps descended the walk. And then they must have made themselves unperceivable to mortal eyes again, because a moment later Loki had glided up to meet us.

"Everything's in order," he said. "He seemed to warm up to the foster parents right away." There was a murmur of cloth I realized was his hand squeezing Ari's shoulder. "You won this battle, pixie."

She shifted, leaning into his touch. Just for a second, but it was enough to turn the ache in my chest into a sliver of jealousy. When had the two of them gotten so familiar?

"I want to stay a little longer," Ari said. "Then we can go kick those dark elf asses."

Loki chuckled. "We'll go finish preparing for *that* battle."

"Are you coming, brother?" Baldur asked.

I shook my head. "I'll return with the valkyrie."

When they'd left, Ari eased her legs down again and leaned back on her hands with a soft creak of the roof. "You don't have to stay," she said. "I didn't go through all this just to screw it up acting stupid now. I just... want to be near him a little more."

"I'm not worried about you doing anything rash," I said. "Do you *want* to be alone?"

She paused. "No," she admitted. "Not really."

We sat for a stretch in silence. Every slight movement she made sent a reverberation through me. I had to say something more.

"I'm sorry."

Her head jerked around with a hiss of her hair. "For what?"

"For suggesting you were selfish. And for— I've been hard on you since the start. I can admit I misjudged you. Loki made a good choice this once, picking you."

She was quiet so long I thought I might have inadvertently offended her more. Then she said, in a tone that suggested a smile, "Okay. Apology accepted. And it's a good thing you feel that way, because it seems like you all are stuck with me now."

"Is that a bad thing?" I asked.

"No, maybe not. I mean, considering the alternatives... Thank you, for being there for Petey and for making this work."

"I know how much it mattered to you. You haven't really left him alone."

"Yeah." She rubbed her hand across her mouth. "Now that you know all my tragic secrets, do you figure someday you'll tell me your sob story? It seems only fair."

The corner of my mouth twitched up even as my gut twisted. "I don't know. Not right now. Maybe someday."

"Well, whenever you're ready, I'm prepared to rage on your behalf."

I snorted, but the words brought back the earlier ache. I had a feeling she would rage, if I let her. But I hadn't even let myself, not ever.

There was something relieving about knowing I'd have someone who'd shout alongside me if I ever felt the need to, though.

Without letting myself second-guess the moment, I slid my hand across the shingles until my fingers brushed Ari's. I gripped them gently. She didn't pull away.

"Someday," she repeated, and hesitated. "I slept with Loki."

A prickling sensation shot through me from head to toe. My back tensed, but I managed to keep my hold on her hand loose and my voice even. "Why are you telling me?"

"Well, I'm sure you'd have figured it out before very long anyway. And I kind of wondered if it'd matter to you."

"It isn't really my business," I said, wondering how much of my reaction she'd already been able to read. "If you want to be with him that way, I'm not going to judge." Not her, anyway. Him, I could fantasize about strangling a little more often than usual.

She hummed to herself. "The other thing is, it's not just about him. I feel connected to the four of you. I thought maybe it would go away once I scratched that itch... but if anything I feel it more now. With all of you."

"We summoned you," I said, but I didn't think that covered the feelings she was talking about. The truth was, more and more, I'd been sensing something similar. "In a strange way, I think maybe we all needed you. Or someone like you."

"Strange, huh?"

"Well, I mean..." I wasn't sure I could talk my way out of that one. I settled on the truth. "You're not what we thought we needed in a valkyrie. Clearly we were wrong. It's been a long time, just the five of us and Odin when he's between wanderings. I'm not sure that's been good for anyone."

"So, you're glad I blew in here and shook things up?"

"I'd say so."

"Good." She let out a shaky laugh. "You know, I've slept with a fair number of guys in the last five years. But you're the first person I've let myself cry in front of since I was twelve. So... you can decide whether one counts any less than the other."

I turned my head toward her. I couldn't see her, no, but the shape of her couldn't have been any sharper in my mind. The ache spread to the edges of my ribs, but it wasn't exactly painful in that moment.

Perhaps I'd been something she needed, too. Something she still needed.

I raised my hand to touch her cheek. She set her hand over my fingers, squeezing them. Then she tilted her head and pressed a soft kiss to my palm.

My pulse jittered at the bolt of sensation that shot down my arm, and I moved without any more thinking. My fingers slid into the waves of her hair as I pulled her into a real kiss.

It'd been a long time since I'd kissed anyone.

Passionate dalliances weren't really my domain. But my mouth seemed to know exactly how to move against Ari's to send a tremor of pleasure through my body and draw a pleased murmur from her throat.

She kissed me back, her hand coming to rest on my neck. The shadows in me stirred in harmony with the dark power contained in her spirit, but she wasn't all dark. Not by a longshot. A brilliance like the sun twined through that darkness, all the warmth and vigor she could bring to bear too. Our dark valkyrie was full of light.

When her mouth slipped away from mine, it was only so she could rest her head on my shoulder. She grasped my hand again, tightly.

"I guess we'd better get going. That battle isn't going to fight itself."

"No, as convenient as that would be."

"The rest... We can figure that all out afterward, right?"

She said it easily, but she tensed a little against me at the same time, as if she was uncertain of my answer. As if the wrong answer would hurt.

I had power here too.

I squeezed her hand back, my voice dropping low. "I'm not going anywhere."

It seemed that was the right answer. Her body relaxed. She pushed herself to her feet and turned toward her brother's new home again.

"Be happy, Petey," she said, and blew a kiss toward the house. Then she spun around.

"Let's fly."

25

Ari

We came to a stop, hovering a few miles from the town that held the dark elves' gate—if it could even be called a town. I could make out only a few dozen wooden buildings, all of them in pretty bad repair. A couple of roofs were caved in, others sagging. Weeds were sprouting up all through the gravel road.

The short, stout figures of the dark elves moved between the buildings here and there, but I didn't see any people. Couldn't taste anything but that sluggish oily energy the elves gave off.

"I don't think anyone human has lived there for a long time," I said.

"A ghost town," Thor said, smacking his hammer against his palm in anticipation. "As good a place for the gate as any."

"I don't see any gate," Muninn said, cocking her head in that bird-like way she had.

"It's there." Freya pointed to a patch of trees on the hillside. Her mouth twisted. "I can feel the chill of the caves even from here."

Loki spun his curved dagger in the air with a sharp grin. "Then into the chill we'll go."

I had my switchblade at the ready, but it was mostly my valkyrie life-taking ability I'd be relying on. Hod had already gathered more shadows to curl around his lean arms and solid chest. Baldur stood ready on the glowing patch of magic that had carried him here, an opposite match for his twin like always.

"Getting to the gate should be the easier part," Freya reminded us. The goddess of love and war looked as stunningly beautiful as ever, but a fierce light gleamed in her eyes that I wouldn't have wanted to go up against. She was carrying a short sword, though I knew it was her magic she planned to do most of her fighting with. "Inside the caves, we'll be more vulnerable. We plow through them as quickly as we can, find our way to Odin, and get out. No stopping for any fancy business."

She didn't look at anyone in particular, but Loki pressed his hand to his breastbone in mock dismay. "No need to doubt me. I shall make my kills clean and swift."

"Are we all ready?" Thor asked in his low voice.

I dragged in a breath and nodded with the others. I still didn't know what the dark elves had meant by the markings they'd left across the country, but I didn't need to. They'd kidnapped the father of the gods, they'd threatened my little brother, and they'd nearly killed me the first chance they had. No, I wasn't going to feel the slightest twinge of conscience over battering our way through them today.

"Baldur?" Freya said.

The bright god raised his hands. His muscular shoulders flexed. "On your command."

We dove down toward the ghost town so fast the wind shrieked in my ears. A shriek rang out below us too as the illusion that had hidden us fell away and a dark elf spotted us.

"Now!" Freya cried.

Baldur heaved his arms forward with all his might, and a searing wave of light swept out ahead of our charge. It hissed through every building, every body, knocking the dark elves flat on their backs with their eyes scorched black. A more fitting color for their personalities, really.

We plummeted past them and raced through the trees where Freya had sensed the gate. The opening was nothing but a wide crack in the rocky mountainside, but an eerie energy emanated from it over my skin. What lay on the other side wasn't earthly at all.

We ran into it without hesitation, Freya and Thor at the lead. I plunged into crashing black darkness that spat me out into a dim, damp cave like the one Valhalla's doorway had led me to.

Thor was already barreling ahead, roaring with anger and swinging his hammer. Sharp slices of Freya's magic hummed through the air. The few dark elves who'd been near the gate when they'd emerged lay crumpled by the walls.

I raced after them alongside the others. Our force burst from the passage into a wider cavern.

A horde of dark elves rushed to meet us, teeth bared and knives hissing. Baldur whipped more streaks of light at them, but his power seemed dampened here, their resistance stronger. Thor's hammer sang through the air. With every crash of it, more elves poured in. Loki lashed out with his dagger, quick and sharp as he'd promised, flames licking over his other hand.

Where the hell was Odin in this place? Several openings branched off from the larger cave, all of them equally shadowed. I swooped over the elvish army, snatching up shudders of life energy through my fingertips with each flap of my wings, but an uneasy stirring rose up from my gut. We were lost. Something was missing.

I couldn't have explained the sensation, but I couldn't shake it either.

Then Muninn cried out where she'd soared in a circle around the outskirts of the room. She pointed with her knife. "This way! The Allfather is this way!"

The gods pushed together in one mass, bashing and blazing a path to the passage she'd pointed to. A dark elf sliced through one of Hod's shadows, but I caught his hair and his life with one hand. Hod aimed another wallop of darkness at an elf that threw herself at my wings. I dove past him with a grateful brush of his shoulder, just in time to see a swarm of our attackers all launch themselves at Thor.

He heaved his hammer toward them, but blood gleamed where blades sank into his thigh, his back. I threw myself forward, snatching at the elves his swing couldn't reach. My arm collided with his brawny body, but one attacker crumpled before he could jab his knife even deeper. The other I kicked away into the next arc of Thor's weapon.

The thunder god caught my gaze for one warm instant. Electricity crackled in his eyes, his face flushed with the heat of the battle, but he offered a quick nod of appreciation despite that.

I didn't have time to enjoy that brief moment of thanks. As we pressed on into the narrower passage, the elves came at us at a furious pace. I could barely get a strong enough hold to tear a life away. For several pulse-thumping minutes, I resorted mostly to stabs of my switchblade and the impact of my elbows and knees. It didn't matter whether they lived or died as long as I kept them off of us.

A dank smell closed in around us, with just a thread of that rot I'd smelled in the caves before. We took another turn, and another, Muninn calling out the way, but the uneasy feeling sank deeper inside me. We *were* missing something. I was sure of it. But damned if I knew what.

Maybe that impression was just some sly magic of the elves. None of the gods seemed to have noticed anything wrong.

We spilled out into another larger cavern, and the raven woman let out a victory cry. There he sat: the Allfather, the tall bearded figure I'd glimpsed in a memory that couldn't be mine as I'd gazed at his throne in Valhalla. But it wasn't a throne the dark elves had given him. Chains twisted all around his body, binding him to the spear of stone he was braced against. His head hung low, bruised and bloodied. I didn't think he was even conscious.

Freya's voice pealed out, ragged and furious. She swept forward, her sword gleaming alongside the slashes of her magic. Thor charged after her. He slammed his hammer against the side of the rock where one of the chains crossed it, and both stone and metal shattered.

Loki darted in to catch Odin as the Allfather sagged forward with the slipping of his bonds. The trickster waved off Thor, making a motion as if to indicate the brawnier god should keep swinging his hammer instead. Baldur slipped through the chaos to support his father's weight on the other side. A healing glow seeped from him into the slumped figure as we reversed the direction of our assault.

My heart thumped frantic but almost giddy. All we needed was to get out. Back out into the sun and fresh air. I could almost taste it ahead of us.

Finding Odin had renewed all the gods' spirits. Loki's flames sizzled through the dark elves and Hod's shadows whipped after them, toppling our attackers in every direction. They pushed forward with a fresh burst of speed, and I found myself bringing up the rear of our battalion. I jabbed my blade and snatched out at flickers of life as the remaining dark elves charged after us.

We'd just broken back out into the first massive cavern, only it and one more tunnel between us and the brighter realm ahead, when a peal of laughter pierced through the grunts and clangs of the battle. My body went rigid, my wings stuttering in mid-flap.

It was Petey's laughter.

The sound that should have been joyful was chilling here. It echoed off the cavern walls, rising and expanding as another elf must have taken up the sound, and another, and another. Suddenly it seemed as if Petey's laughter was ringing out at me from all sides, from hundreds of mouths.

They were reminding me of their threat. Reminding me of what they'd do to him if they found him. Hod had promised he'd wiped the memories of all the dark elves who'd been watching nearby, but obviously there were plenty of others who knew.

Panic clutched my chest. I kicked out at a dark elf that grabbed at my ankle, but the motion felt sluggish, as if I were moving through water.

They were going to come for him. They were going to come for Petey and wrench him with those groping hands and gnashing teeth. How could I think, how could I fight—?

My frantic gaze darted across the room and connected with Loki's. His arm was still braced around Odin, his dagger slashing at the attackers around him, but he met my eyes and mouthed two words.

They lie.

He couldn't know that. He couldn't know anything about what was happening to Petey right now or would happen later. But resolve rose up inside me, breaking through the panic.

I knew. I knew the gods had done everything they

could for Petey, that they'd continue watching out for him after we escaped here. I trusted that if anything could keep him safe, it was the plan we'd already put in place.

And to make sure of that, we *had* to escape.

I let out a cry of my own, rough with fury. My valkyrie power surged through my veins. There was nothing scary about it now. It was pure strength, resonating through me.

At a lash of my knife hand, lightning streaked through several elvish bodies, toppling them. I dove from side to side, severing a throat with a jerk of my blade, letting the coiled darkness inside me swallow life from another attacker. My wings beat the air with a rush of energy. My body moved faster than it ever had before, the enchanted hammer sparked through the air, Loki's flames danced—and the dark elves fell back around us. They stumbled to a stop amid the littered bodies and let us go.

Thor pummeled his way through another surge of attackers on our way down the last cave. Freya took a blow to her face that split her perfect lips. But we made it. We heaved ourselves forward with a final burst of might and spilled into the gate, through the blackness beyond, and out onto soft grass beneath warm sunlight.

26

Ari

Odin staggered as his feet hit the softer ground. All of the gods pulled close in an instant. Muninn grasped the Allfather's arm, looking up at him with hopeful eyes. Loki gave him a fond but careful slap on the back.

"Take us home, brother. Before those cave-dwellers decide to tear after us out here."

The Allfather nodded without a word. He straightened up and raised his arms toward the sky. Light seared up toward the clouds from his hands like a wide blazing rainbow. It burned sharper and clearer until I had no doubt it would hold my feet.

Thor made a triumphant sound and marched forward. Loki and Baldur followed, still offering Odin their support, with Freya and Muninn staying close on either side of him. The Allfather's steps grew steadier as he started to ascend the glowing bridge.

I glanced back toward the gate, but I didn't see any sign that the dark elves had followed us. My body shivered, shedding the tension of the battle.

We'd won. We'd rescued Odin, and maybe soon he'd be able to tell us what else his enemies had been planning and why they'd imprisoned him, and then we could win against them all over again. But even though most of me suddenly felt ten times lighter, my heart beat in my chest with a heavy thud.

That was all true, but I was also leaving my real home behind. Maybe there wasn't that much I'd miss about it, maybe there wasn't much room for me there now, but it had at least been *mine*.

Petey was here, with the new family we'd secreted him away to. My last glimpse of him, his little blond hair disappearing through the doorway of that house, rose up behind my eyes, and a lump filled my throat. I could go to him instead. I could be there, somehow or other...

No. My hands clenched at my sides. We'd gotten Odin back from the dark elves, but they were still here. They still remembered me and Petey. I couldn't put him back in danger.

Hod had started after the others, but he paused and turned back toward me. "Valkyrie?" he said.

His attention no longer felt like a demand. I knew I had to go, at least for now. Exhaling, I set one foot and then the other on the glittering arch. But that didn't feel quite right either.

If I was going as a valkyrie, I might as well fly like one.

I pushed a little into the air and flapped after the others. Hod walked on with a small but soft smile. Seeing it, even the pressure in my chest eased a little.

I was finding a place among gods and giants, a place that maybe I'd be able to call mine eventually. There was plenty to look forward to ahead of me.

The landscape beneath us turned hazy and then faded away into pure blue sky. A golden arc came into view up ahead. Everyone picked up their pace at the sight of it. *Asgard*, I thought, with a tingle of anticipation.

We emerged from beneath the arc into a vast square laid with marble tiles. A gleaming stone building that must have stretched as long as a football field loomed at our right—Valhalla, I guessed. Somehow it didn't command quite the same awe in me from the outside as it had when I'd walked through its dining hall, but it was impressive all the same.

Smaller—but not exactly tiny—stone structures stood farther in the distance, beyond an epic fountain with a dozen cascades of shimmering water gurgling down it. A warm breeze ruffled the feathers on my wings, smelling warm and sweet as honey.

"Oh!" Thor said, stretching his arms. "It's good to be back."

"Everything looks in order," Baldur said with a smile.

"Not much likely to happen to it when no one can get in," Loki pointed out. "But it is good to see Ari didn't throw any wild parties while she had the place to herself." He aimed a wink at me.

"We'll have to choose a house for you," Freya said, looking at me as she brushed her hand across her husband's temple. "No need for you to hang out in that empty war hall. There are quite a few places available— we'll take a little tour and you can pick your favorite."

"That sounds... that sounds really good," I said, and found myself beaming back at her.

Odin's head had twitched to the side at my voice. Thor took his arm with a warm grin at me.

"You haven't gotten to properly meet your newest valkyrie yet, Odin. She's already done you proud."

The Allfather listed a little to the side as he swiveled to face me. Before I'd thought one of his eyes was swollen shut, but I realized it was sealed with a gouge of a scar. An old one from the looks of it, not anything I guessed the dark elves had done to him considering that no one else had commented on it.

His other eye traveled over me with only a vague focus. His shoulders were still stooped. A prickle of the uneasiness I'd felt in the caves crept through me again. He'd been battered by the elves, but shouldn't he be recovering now that he was home too? He was a god like the others. Baldur had lent him healing energy.

"It's because of her that we found you," Hod was saying at Odin's other side. "We sent her up to Valhalla, and she followed Yggdrasil's path to determine who was holding you."

The prickle deepened with a chill that seeped right through my skin. Yes. I'd followed Odin's call to that other doorway to the caves. I'd been able to sense him out there, the god of all valkyries.

I couldn't sense anything like that now, even though he was standing just five feet away from me.

Loki had sauntered over to us. His gaze traveled from me to Odin, and a shadow flickered through his eyes. He turned on his heel.

"Where has that raven gotten to?"

Muninn must have slipped away while everyone was reveling in their relief at being home. But I didn't really care about her. What mattered was the god in front of me.

I stepped closer to Odin and rested my hand over his. Warmth thrummed across his skin, but my valkyrie senses reached deeper. A pulse of energy met my search: a thin, cool energy that made me shiver.

It didn't feel like the warm glow the other gods carried. It barely even felt *alive.*

I wrenched my hand back. "This isn't Odin."

Everyone in the courtyard stiffened. Freya frowned and touched Odin's shoulder gently. "Dearest?"

"Father? Did the dark elves do something to you?" Baldur asked, his smooth face creasing with worry.

Odin started to shake. His hair crumbled, and then his skull, and on and on, his entire form disintegrating into a pile of ash. In the space of a breath, the figure we'd thought was the Allfather was gone.

Freya shrieked and pressed her hand to her mouth. Her other hand closed tight around her sword. Thor let out a growl and raised his hammer, searching the courtyard for an enemy to pummel. Loki's gaze skimmed across the grounds more calmly, but his mouth had set into a hard flat line.

"Only Odin can open the bridge to Asgard," he said. "So if that's not Odin... where in the nine realms are we?"

ABOUT THE AUTHOR

Eva Chase lives in Canada with her family. She loves stories both swoony and supernatural, and strong women and the men who appreciate them. Along with the Their Dark Valkyrie series series, she is the author of the Witch's Consorts series, the Dragon Shifter's Mates series, the Demons of Fame Romance series, the Legends Reborn trilogy, and the Alpha Project Psychic Romance series.

Connect with Eva online:
www.evachase.com
eva@evachase.com